THE BLACKSTONE BAD DRAGON

ALSO BY ALICIA MONTGOMERY

ABOUT THE AUTHOR

Alicia Montgomery has always dreamed of becoming a romance novel writer. She started writing down her stories in now long-forgotten diaries and notebooks, never thinking that her dream would come true. After taking the well-worn path to a stable career, she is now plunging into the world of self-publishing.

f facebook.com/aliciamontgomeryauthor

twitter.com/amontromance

BB bookbub.com/authors/alicia-montgomery

THE BLACKSTONE BAD DRAGON

BLACKSTONE MOUNTAIN BOOK 2

ALICIA MONTGOMERY

CHAPTER 1

Four Weeks Ago...

Pretending to be his twin brother was something Jason Lennox was very good at.

Even now, as he sat in his brother's office, no one had suspected he wasn't Matthew. Not the security guard who greeted him this morning as he entered the lobby. Not the people in the elevator who had given him nervous nods. Not even some of the long-time employees of Lennox Corp. People mixed him and Matthew up all the time, so acting like his cool, more aloof twin was just a matter of switching his personality.

No one could tell them apart, not even their parents or sister, though as they grew older and developed their own separate interests and personalities, people started to notice the difference. Matthew was inclined to stay in his room and finish his homework—even on a Friday night,—while he preferred the company of his friends. Matthew was more serious, which is why he was chosen to be CEO of Lennox Corporation when their mother retired. But he wasn't resentful or anything. He didn't want that responsibility. He preferred running the Lennox Foundation and working in the blackstone mines in his dragon form. His inner dragon loved nothing more than being free. And he couldn't do that if he was stuck in board meetings all day.

Still, despite their differing personalities, the two were as close as anyone could be. Jason would do anything for Matthew. Pretending to be him for the day to help save his twin's reputation and the family company was easy enough.

While he couldn't analyze spreadsheets and stock reports like his brother, he could get by for just a day. When the staff looked at him in his immaculate suit and tie, hair groomed back perfectly and a cool expression on his face, it was easy to fool them into believing he was Matthew. *Easiest gig in the world.*

The phone on the desk rang, and he quickly picked it up. "Matthew Lennox," Jason answered.

"It's me." *Matthew.*

"Oh good." The tension fell from his shoulders and put his feet up on the large oak desk. "What's happening? She's okay, right?"

And this was the reason he was pretending to be his twin. Matthew's mate, Catherine, had been injured following an attack by a pride of lions who had been trying to kill her. Matthew was able to save her in time, but she'd been badly hurt. He couldn't leave her side, which is why Jason had to stand in for him at work. He just hoped she would pull through because it would destroy Matthew if anything happened to her, plus, Jason happened to actually like Catherine. She was a good person.

"Yeah ... she's stable," Matthew said.

"So, what's wrong?" Jason asked, sensing his twin's distress.

"Well, you see ... it turns out Catherine has family. A sister. We met and things didn't go too well. She blames me for what happened and she's trying to take her away."

"Fuck, no!" Jason swiveled the leather chair around and got to his feet. "She can't do that. What do we gotta do to stop her?"

"That's why I called. She left the hospital to grab some things from her hotel room and is coming back soon. You have to delay her somehow."

"And how am I going to do that?"

"I don't know, just ... pretend to be me. Intercept her at the lobby and tell her you're sorry about today and that you just want to talk to her. Charm her. Make her think like you're on her side and that you're not trying to stop her. We just need some time to get into Catherine's room so I can talk to her."

"Ah," Jason said with a nod. "Gotcha."

"Oh and by the way—shit!" Matthew cursed. "Sorry, Jason, I gotta go."

And so an hour and a half later, he arrived at the lobby of The Ritz Ski Resort, just thirty miles out of Blackstone town. He sat in one of the wingback chairs, nursing a whiskey as he scanned the area for ... what was her name? Christina. Matthew had forgotten to tell him what this Christina looked like. He supposed if she was related to Catherine, they would look alike. Would she be pretty? Jason let out a snort. Who cares? If she was trying to take Catherine away, then Jason would do whatever it took to stop her. Even if she looked like the Wicked Witch of the West, he would do his best to charm her, at the very least, distract her long enough for Matthew to convince Catherine they were mates and make her stay with him forever.

He let out another snort and swirled the crystal glass in his hand before taking another sip. Not that he wasn't happy for his twin. Matthew was finally getting that stick out of his ass, and that was all thanks to Catherine. Dragons rarely found mates, after all. Matthew's dragon not only recognized Catherine as his mate, but also confirmed a legend from their mom's side of the family.

Their mother, Riva, told them of a saying from the Sinclair family: the one who knows you from your twin is your soul mate. And it seemed Matthew had indeed found his. Jason wouldn't have believed it if he hadn't seen it himself. Despite seeing them side-by-side, Catherine didn't believe they were twins. In fact, she said they looked different in her eyes. Jason had found her cute, even flirted with her, but backed off quickly when it became obvious Matthew's dragon had already staked its claim.

Good for him. Having a mate was something his brother needed. Someone to lean on during the tough times, and of course, have cute little dragonlings who would carry on the family name. If he had to name one reason to be glad about not being the heir to Lennox Corp., it would be that he was free. Free to do whatever he wanted. And whomever he wanted. In fact—he was antsy now. He hoped this wouldn't take too long, because all he wanted was to head over to The Den and find some friendly company for the evening. Someone new and exciting. There was nothing like the thrill of the chase, the feel of a gorgeous woman in his bed. And—

The glass in his hand dropped with a soft thud, spilling the amber contents onto plush, white carpet. But he didn't notice it; in fact, the entire room seemed to quiet down as he stared ahead. His heart began to hammer against his rib cage.

She walked into the lobby of The Ritz like she was a queen, like she owned it. Dressed in a white wool coat, stiletto heels, and wearing a cool expression on her beautiful face. A very familiar face.

"Goddamn Matthew." His brother had conveniently forgotten to mention something of importance. Christina wasn't just Catherine's sister. She was her *twin*. But even though they were the spitting image of each other, there was something about her that was different and he couldn't stop staring. She turned her head and ice-blue eyes stared right back at him and in that moment, his heart stopped beating. Everything slowed down and froze.

Mine.

Huh? Jason shook his head.

It was suddenly noisy in the lobby again and time went back to normal speed. But she was still staring at him, and for just a brief second he saw that cool mask disappear. She had seemed surprised to see him, flustered even. *Of course she was,* he told himself. She and Matthew had met earlier and had a nasty confrontation. As her cool demeanor returned, she turned away and began to walk toward the doors.

Shit! Can't let her get away! Jason shot to his feet, threw a couple of bills on the table, and strode after Christina. She was standing by the door, hands on her hips, an impatient look on her face.

"Uhm, Christina," he called as he stopped in front of her. "I'm glad I caught up with you."

She looked up at him, those light-blue eyes pinning him with a frosty gaze. "Excuse me?"

"Look, I came here to apologize. For this morning?" God, he sounded like an idiot. He really should have gotten more details from Matthew.

"What are you talking about? Do I know you?" she asked with a frown. Her accent was posh and elegant, very different from her sister's.

Was this chick on something? "We met this morning and—"

"You must have mistaken me for someone else," she said, then looked away impatiently.

"Wait, you don't know me?" he asked.

She turned back toward him, her gaze perusing him from head to toe. "I don't think so."

Oh no.

Oh hell *no.*

Jason's heart sped up again. *There's got to be some mistake.* "Listen, Christina. I—"

"Please don't address me in such a familiar tone," she snapped. "I told you, I'm not who you think I am."

"Christina…Archer?"

Her eyes narrowed to slits. "It's Stavros," she corrected. "So, obviously, I'm not who you're looking for." She began to walk away from him and headed out the front door.

Mine.

"Shut the fuck up!" he growled at his inner dragon. No, there was some mistake. Christina whatever her name was, was *not* his mate. He didn't want a mate. He didn't *need* a mate. His life was perfectly fine the way it was. Drinking and having fun, and fucking any woman he wanted. "Shit!" As much as he wanted to run in the opposite direction, he'd promised Matthew he would keep her away from the hospital.

As he walked out of the hotel lobby, he told himself there had to be a reasonable explanation. Christina and Catherine shared DNA. *Yeah, that was it.* It didn't mean Christina was his mate. It couldn't, because otherwise, karma was really kicking his ass.

The frigid night air hit his face, but he shrugged it off. He was a shifter, after all, and his own dragon fire could melt all the snow on the mountains. Glancing around, he saw Christina huddled under a heat lamp, arms around herself, and her head glancing up and down the driveway of The Ritz. Shoving his hands into his pockets, he walked over to her.

"Are you following me?" she asked.

"Look, if you'd just let me explain—"

"I told you ... Wait." Her eyes lit up in recognition. "I think I know who you are."

A spark of hope lit up in Jason, and he ignored his dragon's protests.

"You're the new driver that the car company sent," she said. "The dispatcher said she'd be sending someone new, since my driver was called away."

"Yeah?" *Driver?*

The expression on her face turned from anger to relief. "Oh, that must be it." She frowned. "I wish you'd identified yourself sooner. Don't you have ID or something?"

"I ... lost it," he said. Okay, so she thought he was a limo driver. He'd take that. After all, mate or not (and definitely not), he had a job to do. He couldn't let Matthew down. "Uhm, so yeah, where'd you want to go?"

"To Blackstone Hospital," she said, placing her hands on her hips. "Well?"

He didn't realize he'd been staring at her. How could he not? Standing this close to her, he could see how smooth and porcelain-like her skin was. Her cheeks were pink from the heat of the lamp and her blue eyes shone like crystal. There was just something about her that made him want to stare for hours.

"Right," he cleared his throat. "I'll get the car."

Jason walked across the parking lot, then climbed into his jacked up Chevy Silverado. Shit, if he knew he'd be playing chauffeur, he would have taken one of the company cars. At least his truck looked shiny and new. Not exactly something a limo company would have, but he'd just have to come up with some excuse.

He maneuvered the truck to the driveway, slipped out, and walked around to open the door for Christina.

"*This* is the car?" she asked, raising a delicate brow.

He nodded toward the road, which was icy and covered in snow. "That's why they sent me," he said. *Good save.* "Look lady, if you want a fancy limo or something, you can wait until morning. But in these conditions, you'll need my truck."

She hesitated for a moment. "Fine." She climbed up, though the truck was so high, it was a feat in her skinny stilettos and tight skirt suit, though she managed it with grace. Jason tried not to stare at the perfectly-formed ass as she got inside. With a cheeky grin and a tip of an imaginary hat, he closed the door and walked over to the driver's side.

Okay, gotta think about how to keep her away, Jason thought as he slipped back into the vehicle. He glanced at the rearview mirror. Christina was staring outside, her face drawn into a worried expression. Of course she was anxious. Her twin sister had been shot and fighting for her life. If that had happened to Matthew, he'd be worried too. He wished he could reach out and smooth that wrinkle between her eyebrows.

"*Ahem.*" Christina was staring back at him.

"Right," he said, regaining his composure. "Let's go."

"So," he began. "Why'd you choose to stay here if you needed to go to the hospital? Seems so far away."

She let out an impatient sigh. "My assistant made the reservation. She said that with the tourist season in Blackstone, all the hotels in the area were booked up."

"Ah, I see. And why'd you come all the way to Blackstone?"

"It's a private matter," she replied. "And I'd prefer to keep it that way." She looked away, crossing her arms, and looked out the window.

"Sorry," he murmured. There was no way this cold, stuck-up human was his mate, unless fate really did hate him. *Okay, no more small talk.* But, he needed a plan.

An idea popped into his head. She wasn't going to like it, but she probably wasn't going to like anything he came up with.

He continued along the main highway down the mountain. It was late enough that it was practically deserted. No other car had passed their way. Thanks to his shifter sight, he spotted a smaller road in the distance veering off gently. He made the detour, glancing up at the rearview mirror, but Christina stared down at her phone, fingers tapping on the screen rapidly. With a frustrated sigh, she put the phone back into her purse.

"Everything okay?" he asked.

"Yes. I mean, no." She shook her head. "I just lost reception on my phone. I was replying to my father. Anyway..." She frowned and looked around. "I don't recall leaving the main road when we drove up here before."

"It's a shortcut," he said. "Don't worry about it."

He drove for a couple of minutes, hoping the road

wouldn't end soon. The problem was these types of mountain roads usually ventured off into private property or a dead-end. Either way, they would have to turn back. He needed another excuse to stall.

Then, inspiration hit him. He began to ease his foot off the gas, allowed the car slow to a stop then turned the ignition off.

"Uh-oh," he feigned.

"Uh-oh?" Christina said. "What do you mean, *uh-oh?*"

"Well, this hasn't happened in a long while." He pretended to turn the key in the ignition several times.

"What's going on?" she asked, her voice rising.

"It's nothing, don't worry," he reassured her, opening the door and sliding out.

"Don't worry? I—"

He shut the door before she could protest further. She *really* wasn't going to like this.

Jason walked to the front of the truck and lifted up the hood. Christina couldn't see him, so he stood there, pretending to look into the engine and trying to come up with some excuse. Finally, he put the hood down and hopped back into the truck.

"Well?" Christina asked, her eyes narrowed at him.

He shook his head. "The engine's shot."

"What do you mean? It was just fine a while ago."

"Yeah, well, cars are funny like that," he said, mentally crossing his fingers and hoping she didn't know shit about engines. "Must be the cold weather. Wasn't expecting it and the, uh, driver before me didn't fill up the antifreeze."

"Well, what are you going to do about it?" she asked. "Did you call your dispatcher? Your boss?"

"Yeah, about that…" He held up his phone. "No reception either. You have any luck with yours?"

Christina grabbed her phone from her purse and tapped on the screen. "Ugh. No."

"Well then," he said, settling into the seat. "I guess we'll have to wait."

"Excuse me? Wait here?" He could practically see the steam coming out from her ears. If she wasn't human, she would have made a great dragon. "We're in the middle of nowhere! Shouldn't we get help?"

"Lady, it's freezing out there." He pointed to her stilettos. "Are you going to be walking around dark mountain roads in those?"

"I…I…" Her face turned red. "Then what are *you* going to do?"

"You think I'm going out there?" he looked back at her incredulously and shook his head. "We'll stay here. When my dispatcher doesn't hear from us in an hour or two, she'll send someone to check. Don't worry," he reassured her. "This happens occasionally. We have systems in place for every eventuality." He reclined the seat, closed his eyes, and relaxed. "We just have to wait it out."

He heard her make an irritated huffing sound, then a resigned sigh. She shuffled around and when he turned to glance back at her, she had settled against the corner of the backseat, her coat draped over her, and legs tucked underneath. For a moment, Jason felt a surge of desire, watching her beautiful, peaceful face. He ignored it and closed his eyes.

Jason woke up later, jolted from sleep by the sound of something…chattering? Jason sat up, rubbed his eyes, and looked back.

Christina was lying down on the backseat. Her wool coat

was draped over her like a blanket, but it was too short. Even curled up, her legs stuck out. The temperature must have dropped significantly in the last three hours, but he didn't notice because his shifter biology kept him warm.

His dragon roared in anger. *Damn animal.* Still, an ache pressed into his gut, seeing her cold and knowing it was his fault. She could get sick, if she wasn't already. *Fuck*, he cursed inwardly. Without thinking, he slipped out the driver's side and climbed into the backseat.

Jason nudged her over then draped her legs over his lap. "Jesus," he muttered. Her shapely legs were ice-cold. He glanced at her face to check on her, but she didn't wake up. In fact, she let out a sigh and moved lower, pressing her ass against his side and curling her legs over his lap, seeking his warmth. He let out a groan as his cock stood at attention and adjusted his pants. He had to ignore the desire clawing at him because there was no way he was going to give in to it.

Jason wasn't sure how long they'd been in the car, but by the time he opened his eyes, there was light outside. But that wasn't what sent his senses into overdrive. No, it was the warm, soft body pressed up against him and the delicious, sweet scent that was threatening to overwhelm him.

His body stiffened and he looked down. A warm cheek lay against his chest, soft tendrils of blonde hair covering him. Quiet snores came from pink, parted lips. Even asleep, Christina was gorgeous, her face peaceful and calm.

They somehow must have shifted positions in the night, because he was now on his back and Christina was draped over him. She snuggled deeply against him, seeking his warmth.

He thought he groaned inwardly, but he must have done it loudly enough to wake her up. Her eyes flew open. Light-blue pools blinked up at him contentedly, but as she seemed to realize where she was, her expression changed as quick as lightning.

Christina scrambled to her knees, gathering her wool coat against her chest like a shield, and scooted to the other end of the seat. She looked furious. Her eyes blazed like hot blue flames and her face flushed. "What … how … how dare you!"

"What?" he asked nonchalantly. "I came back here because you were cold and put your legs over me. You were the one who wanted to cuddle."

He didn't think it was possible, but she got even redder. "I did not!"

Jason shrugged. "Hey, nothing happened. Are you embarrassed or something?" He pointed to a wet spot on his shirt. "You don't have to worry, babe. What's a little drool between friends?"

She let out an indignant sound and looked like she was about to claw his eyes out, when a tapping sound on the window made them both freeze. Jason turned around and saw a uniformed figure outside the car. Recognizing who it was, he immediately opened the door.

"Hey, Cole," he greeted.

Deputy Police Chief Cole Carson gave him a strange look. "Mornin', Jason," he greeted. Cole was two years ahead of Jason in high school, but they both played on the football team for Blackstone High. Cole had been the star quarterback and would have gone pro if they allowed shifters in the leagues. Instead, he went military, then came back to join

Blackstone P.D. "Is everything okay here?" He leaned down, and when his eyes landed on Christina, gave her a nod. "Mornin', ma'am."

Jason's dragon nearly ripped out of him, wanting to tear Cole apart for even looking at Christina. Cole's bear hadn't missed it, based on his now-glowing eyes. Jason could feel the dominant creature inside Cole roaring to get out, ready for a fight.

Cole stepped back. "Jesus, buddy, quit it!"

Jason reared his dragon back, willing it to calm down. Cole didn't stand a chance against him, but this was insane. His dragon was never a violent creature. He shook his head. "Sorry, man, I'm just a little disoriented."

Cole's eyes returned to normal. "Car trouble?"

"Yeah, just … something with the engine."

"Officer," Christina said in a sweet voice. "Thank God you found us. I thought we would have frozen to death before we got rescued."

"Seems mighty unusual, you getting stuck out here."

Shit. It was obvious Cole knew something was up. "Yeah, well, you never know how these things go," Jason quickly added.

Cole raised a brow, but said nothing. "Can I give you both a ride?"

"Oh, that would be wonderful, Officer…"

"Carson. Deputy Police Chief Cole Carson."

"Deputy Carson," Christina said as she slipped on her heels and yanked the door lever open. "Do you think you could take me to Blackstone Hospital?"

"Uhm, that's not really my—"

"Oh please?" She gave him a megawatt smile. "I'd really

appreciate it" Her voice became breathy. "It's an emergency. I have to check and see if my sister is out of her coma."

Jason realized what she was doing and his fingers nearly ripped into the leather seats of his truck, but he stopped himself before he could do any damage. He'd just had them redone a month ago. Besides, the only thing that would sate his dragon now was punching Cole's face in. *Poor fool*, he convinced himself. He couldn't see she was only flirting with him to get what she wanted.

"Well, I *am* going into town," Cole said. "Let me pull my car over. You really shouldn't be walking around in the ice and snow in those heels." With a tip of his hat, he turned back toward the cruiser. When he was gone, Christina scrambled out of the truck and slammed the door hard.

"Goddamnit," Jason cursed as he followed after her. She was already walking toward the police car when he grabbed her arm. "Christina, wait—"

"Don't touch me," she said, jerking away. "Something's going on here. I can *feel* it." Her eyes narrowed at him. "You're not a driver, are you?"

Damn. Gorgeous *and* smart. He was even more turned on. He put on a smile and gave her a wink. "What do you think?"

Her expression turned to controlled fury. "Frankly, I don't care. After today, I'll never see this stupid little town ever again. Don't even think of getting into that car with me or I'll tell Deputy Carson what you did and have him arrest you for impersonating my driver. I hope I never see you again!" She whipped around, yanked the door to the police car open and stepped inside. "He says he has to wait here for someone," he heard her say to Cole. "We can go, Deputy."

Jason watched the black-and-white pull away from him.

Shit. Hopefully Matthew had worked things out with Catherine. He kicked a stone as he walked back to his truck. He should just go home and forget what happened last night, and forget about Christina Stavros. But, as the engine of his truck roared to life, he found himself driving back to town. *Have to make sure Matthew's got his girl*, he told himself. Yeah, that was it.

CHAPTER 2

PRESENT DAY...

"Are you okay?"

Christina turned around, her hands rubbing over her arms, trying to ward off the chill. "I'm fine."

Her stepbrother, Kostas, gave her a skeptical look. "Christina, you don't have to be here for cleanup. You should have gone home with the first transport out. You have a long trip—"

"I said I'm fine." She shrugged. Kostas knew her *too* well. There were few things she could hide from him. "I just want to make sure we get those guys who did this."

"Me too." He put an arm around her. "And we will. Hurting shifters is one thing, but what they were trying to do to those cubs? A thousand slow deaths would be too good. We'll find them."

She nodded. "I know we will."

He gave her a reassuring squeeze. "I have to talk to Anton

and make sure we have enough beds at the facility to take care of everyone. Xander and Father will want to know what's happening as well."

"Go ahead," she said with a nod. Kostas flashed a weak smile then left.

She gave an involuntary shiver. It wasn't the biting cold that made her tremble, but what she had just witnessed. Children inside cages. The brutal conditions in that freezing basement. Those men with the hollow look in their eyes, as if they held no remorse or guilt over what they'd done.

Of course, the moment they burst in, those cowards ran away. Christina didn't even get the chance to knock some heads to take out the frustration that had been building inside her for weeks.

But there would be other chances, of course. There was an abundance of cruelty in the world, especially toward shifters. This shifter smuggling ring was just one group of many. Which is why her adoptive father, Aristotle Stavros, Alpha of the Lykos pack, established the Shifter Protection Agency.

Since governments all over the world would never allow shifters to band together, The Agency had to do their jobs in secret, under the guise of working for Stavros International, Ari's company. Their primary work was to stop those trying to harm shifters. They were a small team and Ari's vast wealth was enough to fund them, allowing them to run operations all over the world, wherever they were needed.

Ari had kept it all a secret from his stepdaughters and their younger half-sister, but Christina had figured it out when she came back from boarding school. Though human herself, she had begged Ari to let her join them. After all, she hated those anti-shifter groups as much as he did. But he had never allowed it. It was only when Catherine had run away and she threatened to do the same that Papa let her join, first as an analyst, and now as a field agent. Kostas and her brothers had been teaching her to defend herself since she was twelve, and now she was able to put some of those skills to good use.

Their intelligence network had heard about this shifter smuggling ring weeks ago, but they didn't know just how bad it was. They weren't just targeting shifters, but their children. There were at least half a dozen wolf and bear cubs in that basement Christina didn't know what they were planning, but she could all too easily imagine. Despite all the savagery she'd seen in the past year as part of The Agency, it still made her furious. She wanted to break something or someone, preferably the heads of whoever was behind this.

"Christina." Nikos, the youngest of her stepbrothers, called her name. He had come up behind her and she didn't even notice.

"Yes?"

"We need to leave now if you're going to make your flight to Colorado."

"*Gamisou*," she cursed under her breath.

Nikos grinned, obviously catching her words with his enhanced hearing. "You've been hanging around us too long. What would Father say if he heard you curse like that?"

"Where do you think I learned?" she retorted. "Not from boarding school, that's for sure." She sighed.

"It's just one week, Christina," he said. "And we'll follow in a few days."

"Right."

One week in Blackstone. In one week, her twin sister would be marrying her dragon. Catherine and Matthew's engagement shouldn't have been a surprise, since they were already mates, but she'd hoped it would be a while before she had to go back. The churning in her stomach wouldn't stop when she thought about going back to Blackstone. Which led to her thinking about that handsome face and those silvery eyes.

Damn Jason Lennox. How could one man have such an effect on her? It had been *weeks* since that night, and still she couldn't stop thinking about him. *That big fat liar. Arrogant asshole.* Catherine had explained why he did what he did, but still …

She shook her head. Just one week. After this week, she'd have to insist that Catherine and Matthew spend some holidays back home in Lykos. Because she had no intention of going back to Blackstone or spending more time around Jason Lennox than necessary.

She looked around her, at the instruments of cruelty and evil littering the basement. This was what she was meant to do. Put a stop to those trying to hurt shifters and their loved ones, so that no parent would ever have to lose a child, and no child would ever grow up without a parent.

It was the vow she made after those evil men murdered her mother.

The flight to Blackstone was uneventful, if long. She wished that the jet could have brought her here, but unfortunately, her father had to finish up some work in China and Korea before the wedding, so she had to fly commercial.

It wasn't that she was too good to fly commercial; she'd done it lots of times, of course. But she preferred the peace and quiet of flying private. No one bothered her unless she needed them. Even waiting at the gate in Heathrow to board had her bristling. Too many people in one small space. The first class cabins on the larger plane to New York gave her some semblance of privacy, but once they reached the US, she had to transfer to a smaller airline to get to Colorado.

The plane that brought Christina into the regional airport outside Blackstone was half-empty and she was grateful for the peace and quiet. A strange, unnerving feeling passed through her as the plane touched down on the runway. Nervousness? Anticipation? She scoffed. *Ridiculous.* There was nothing to be nervous about. Blackstone meant nothing to her. The only connection she had with the place was her sister.

Why Catherine would choose this backwater town as her home was beyond her. They'd grown up on their own private island paradise surrounded by luxury for God's sake. Papa gave them everything they could want or need. Why would anyone give that up and live here? Christina was already dreaming of going for a swim in the Mediterranean. *Yes, that would be nice.* A quick break on Lykos before going back to work. She wouldn't be too long. After all, the bad guys didn't take vacations, why should she?

Christina grabbed her luggage from the carousel and headed toward Arrivals. Her phone had died halfway through the flight and there were no charging ports on that dinky little plane. Still, she wasn't worried as Catherine said she would be picking her up. But, there was no sign of her. In fact, there was only one vehicle, and one person waiting outside as she exited the door.

"Bloody hell," she muttered to herself.

Jason Lennox leaned against the side of his truck, arms crossed over his chest. She bit her lip as she watched the muscles in his shoulders move deliciously under his black T-shirt. Her cheeks went hot when she remembered that morning when she was laying on top of him, pressed against his hard chest. He had been so warm and lying next to him felt wonderful, especially after being in that freezing car for hours. *Which had been all his doing,* she reminded herself. He also had that smile on his face, the same one that infuriated and made her knees go weak at the same time. He had been clean-shaven at the time, but now, the dark stubble on his jaw only made him look more handsome. And dangerous.

"What are you doing here?" she asked in the frostiest tone she could muster. "Where's my sister?"

Silvery eyes bore into her and her heart began to race. "She was called away. Wedding shit." He shrugged. "Sorry, I was the only one who could come and pick you up." He glanced down at her outfit—knee-high leather boots over thick leggings and a lightweight puffy coat. "Glad to see you're dressed for the weather."

"You never know when someone will try to get you stuck in the middle of nowhere and make you freeze to death," she retorted.

His face lit up with amusement. "Don't worry, I only do that when I meet someone for the first time."

She was taken aback by his reaction. Indeed, Jason Lennox wasn't like any man she had met before. Most people were intimidated by her demeanor, but not him. "I could have taken a cab. What are you doing?" He ignored her and was already grabbing her suitcase. "I can do that, you know. I'm not an invalid."

He tossed the luggage into the back of his truck. "C'mon, let's get out of here." He walked over to the passenger side and opened the door. "I'm not playing driver today, so I hope you don't mind staying up front."

"It's fine," she said, climbing in.

"Shouldn't be too long," Jason said as he stepped up into the driver's seat, "and the weather's holding up. Starting to get warmer, too."

"This is *warm*?" she asked, tugging her jacket closer. "It doesn't feel any warmer than my last visit."

He chuckled. "That's because you're not from around here. Of course, you're also human." He flashed her a look from those silvery eyes and her stomach flip-flopped.

"I'm not used to snow or the cold," she said.

"Yeah, Catherine told me," he replied as he drove out of the airport. "You grew up on some Greek island, right?"

"Lykos." She sighed, thinking of the warm sun and the sandy beach.

"You miss it already?"

"I haven't been home in a while. I've been traveling. For work," she added quickly.

"And what is it you do again?"

"I work for the marketing department of Stavros International," she replied. "How long until we get to the hotel?" she said, trying to change the subject.

"Hotel?"

"Yeah, I assumed Catherine booked me at a hotel or something until the wedding. I don't really know any details."

Jason chuckled. "You're not staying at a hotel. You'll be staying at my family's home. Blackstone Castle."

"What?" She swallowed a gulp. "I can't stay with you."

"Who says you're staying with me?" he asked. "I have my own place in town. Unless you'd like—"

"I wasn't implying anything," she said in a defensive tone. "I guess it would be nice to be near Catherine and spend more time with her." She had missed her sister a lot the past year while she'd been away.

"Yeah, I can't imagine being apart from Matthew for so long either," he said.

"Right." Matthew and Jason were apparently twins, too. There must be something in the water in Blackstone because everyone in the town seemed to think they looked alike. Glancing at Jason, she still couldn't figure out how. Matthew was cute, she supposed, but nowhere near as handsome as Jason. Not that she'd ever admit it out loud. Jason had a more defined profile, and his hair was thicker and darker. The eyes were similar, but Matthew's were a dull gray, while Jason's were a bright silver. Matthew looked more like an older cousin than a brother, much less a twin brother.

"You could come back to visit after the wedding," he suggested.

She snorted and stared ahead at the highway. "I'm far too busy," she said. "Besides, there's nothing here apart from my sister that I'd want to come back for."

"Really?" he asked, glancing at her. "Nothing at all?"

"Maybe that hot deputy."

The air went noticeably still and cold in the truck. She whipped her head toward Jason, and though his expression didn't change, his knuckles were bone white as he gripped the wheel. He kept staring ahead, his steely eyes on the road, not saying a word. He took a deep breath, and the atmosphere inside the cab turned back to normal.

Christina leaned back, relaxing as she could now breathe the air. She'd been around shifters, mostly wolves, her whole life, but she'd never experienced *that*. The power emanating from him had been intimidating, and she realized it probably wasn't a good idea to provoke dragons. She wasn't sure why those words came out of her mouth. Maybe she just wanted to shut him up. It apparently worked.

The rest of the ride was silent, and Christina spent the rest of it looking outside, watching the scenery go by. They drove through Blackstone town which she recognized, then wove their way up the mountains to reach their destination.

Her jaw dropped at her first sight of Blackstone Castle. She hadn't been sure what she'd expected, but it certainly wasn't *this*. Catherine had told her it was a castle, but she'd thought her sister was just exaggerating. But no, it was an honest-to-goodness, fairy-tale castle built on a mountain with turrets, stonework, and gothic arches. The snow covering the rooftops made it look like it should be on the cover of a fantasy novel.

"Not bad, huh?" Jason said, his tone amused. "C'mon, I'll show you in."

Christina stared up at Blackstone Castle, drinking in the sight. It was huge and made their luxurious villa on Lykos look small. She didn't want to seem too impressed, but she supposed it was understandable in this situation.

"Let's go," Jason said, marching toward the entrance without waiting for her. By the time Christina caught up to him, the front door was already opening.

"Oh, you're here," the older woman waiting on the other side greeted. She looked at Christina, her smile warm. "You must be Christina. I'm Meg, the housekeeper."

"Nice to meet you," she said politely.

"Meg's more than just our housekeeper," Jason said. "She took care of all of us and made sure we were fed."

"Oh, Jason," she said, laughing and pinching his cheeks. "I only helped when your mom wasn't around, and even that was rare." She turned back to Christina. "Oh my, Catherine told me you were twins, but looking at you..." She shook her head. "You'd think I'd be used to it by now. Anyway, you must be tired or hungry, or both. Let's get you settled into the guest room. Would you mind taking her suitcase up, Jason? I have her in the guest bedroom in the east wing."

Meg motioned for Christina to follow her into the house. The inside of the castle was just as breathtaking, but in a different way. It looked like it had been modernized, but the decor was still in keeping with the castle theme; classic but understated, with a few modern touches here and there. They walked up a large set of stone staircases then turned right down a long hallway.

"The kids—sorry, I still think of them as kids—I mean, Matthew and his siblings have the entire east wing to them-selves," Meg explained. "These days it's just Matthew and Catherine here. The West wing belongs to Jason's parents, Hank and Riva, though they're away on a 'round-the-world trip after they retired. They'll be back for the wedding, of course." They walked down one of the hallways, and stopped at the door at the very end. "This is the guest bedroom. I've prepared it myself so I hope you like it. I asked Catherine if you had any preferences, but she said you weren't picky." She opened the door and stood back to let Christina enter.

"I'm sure I'll have everything I need," she said. The room was spacious and luxurious, with a sitting area in the corner next to floor-to-ceiling windows, and a queen-size canopy bed in the middle.

Meg gave her a reassuring pat on the arm. "Well, if there's anything you need, just ask. I'll send up some refreshments for you, in case you're hungry."

Christina wanted to protest, but had a feeling Meg wouldn't take no for an answer. She thanked the older woman as she left, then turned around to further examine her surroundings.

She headed toward the sitting area, and as she looked out the large window, the view of the mountains outside made her stop. It was gorgeous outside. They were probably quite high up that the snow was still thick on the side of the mountains and on the trees. The sky was a clear blue and in the distance, she saw a large bird circling over the trees.

"Beautiful, huh?"

She nearly jumped out of her skin at the sound of Jason's voice. Glancing behind her, she saw he was by the doorway, carrying her suitcase. She'd forgotten that Meg asked him to bring it up. "You can put that down anywhere. I'll take care of it," she said in a brusque voice.

"You're welcome, by the way," he said through gritted teeth, setting the suitcase by the bed.

She felt blood rush to her cheeks in embarrassment. She wasn't raised to be impolite, but something about him just rubbed her the wrong way. "Thank you," she said in a soft voice. Maybe it wasn't Jason. Maybe it was *her*, and it had been too long since she'd been around people other than her family and teammates at The Agency. She'd cut herself off emotionally from other people for so long. "And I'm sorry for my rudeness," she added.

Jason's face softened into a look she'd never seen before and he moved closer. "Apology accepted. But only if you accept mine," he said in a low voice. "For making you stay in the truck and nearly freezing you to death."

His proximity made her tense, and his words brought back memories of that night. Not of the part where she was shivering because of the cold, but of after. When she was lying on top of him, listening to the beating of his heart, and enjoying the rise and fall of his chest. She had been awake much longer than she cared to admit. "I'm much tougher than I look, Jason," she said with a nervous laugh.

"Hmmm…that's the first time you've said my name." God, was the room getting smaller? And warmer? Or was it because Jason Lennox was leaning toward her, his silvery gaze boring into hers. "I like it."

It was intoxicating, looking up at him, having him so close. "I—"

A loud ringing sound interrupted her and broke the tension in the air. He let out a soft curse and took his phone out of his pocket. *Sorry*, he mouthed as he picked up the call and turned away. "Hello … "

Christina staggered back, unsure of what nearly happened. She blinked several times. No, it was her imagination.

Jason spoke into the phone, his shoulders tensing with each passing second. When he finished, he turned back to her. "I have to go. Trouble at work."

She frowned. "Is everything okay?"

"I'm not sure," he said. "Just ask Meg or any of the staff if you need anything. I don't know when Catherine will be back, but she shouldn't be gone too long."

"I'll give her a call when my phone charges up."

Jason gave her nod and strode toward the door. She thought he hesitated for a moment, but when he left the room, she realized it must have been her imagination acting up again. Like when she thought he was leaning down to kiss her.

"Kiss me?" she said aloud, then shook her head. *I really must be tired*. Her muscles were sore, and she didn't have any rest on the flight. A good nap was in order. Then, she'd be more herself.

CHAPTER 3

JASON STEPPED on the gas and the castle's image shrank rapidly in the rear vision mirror.

Mine, his dragon insisted. *Mine!*

He slammed on the brake halfway down the mountain road leading to the mines. "Shut up!" Goddamn dragon. "She's not ours."

The fucking animal had been a damn asshole the last few weeks. Clawing at him, roaring at him, and fighting him at every turn. And every single time he got near any other woman, it would rail at him. For the first time in his life, he wished the damn thing would just go away.

After weeks of fighting, seeing Christina at the airport finally calmed the dragon down. Catherine called him, saying she had a wedding emergency (whatever that was), and asked if he could pick up Christina. He almost said no, but just the sound of her name soothed his dragon.

He hadn't been sure what to expect when they'd met again. He huffed. He'd wondered if she was still angry, or if she'd felt the same anticipation he had while waiting outside the airport.

Fuck, he was turning into a lovesick idiot, like the ones from those romantic movies. He ran a hand through his hair. He couldn't stop thinking about her, even after all these weeks. And the fact that she seemed immune to whatever it was affecting him made him crazy. She was the same— unfriendly and indifferent. Though apparently, she thought Cole was hot.

No! Mine.

"Quit it!" He nearly lost it, but had the presence of mind to stop himself from losing his temper. He would never hurt her, but he wanted to shake her senseless. Or kiss her so she could forget about Cole or any other man.

A few deep breaths calmed him down and he had enough control to start driving again. Clearing his head, he focused on the task at hand.

The call from Ben had been unnerving. In all the years the mines had been in operation, they'd never had a major acci- dent. Maybe a few minor scrapes, but never one that had injured anyone badly. And now...

He stepped on the gas and drove through the familiar mountain roads, all the way to the blackstone mines, named for the substance found deep inside the mountains. Black- stone was the hardest substance on earth and there was only one way to mine it: dragon fire. Perhaps it was a lucky twist of fate that his four-times grandfather Lucas Lennox won the mountains in a card game. It had made him and his family one of the richest in the country.

Jason made it to the mining site in record time. He parked his car and jogged up to the mouth of the cavern they had dug a few weeks back. Benjamin Walker, his cousin and their lead foreman, was waiting outside, a grim look on his face.

"How bad is it?" Jason asked.

Ben rubbed a hand down his bearded face. "Pretty bad. Good thing we got to them in time. They're on their way to hospital now."

"Show me what happened."

His cousin nodded and led him inside, deeper into the mine. It was dark, but his shifter sight quickly adjusted so he could see around him. Ben directed his attention to the pile of metal and glass in the middle, and the smell of blood hit his nose like a dank perfume.

Mining blackstone was difficult, and turning it into something useful was even harder. The Lennoxes had always hired shifters for the collecting and processing of the blackstone, because they healed faster when they handled the flaming hot rocks. With modern technology, few workers suffered any injuries, though Lennox Corp. still hired shifters to do the more dangerous jobs inside the mines.

"How could this happen?" Jason asked. "We use the best equipment in the world and our safety standards are above average."

Ben shook his head. "We're still looking into it." He nodded toward a group of men huddled in the corner. Nathan Caldwell, their chief engineer, was talking in a low voice to their workers. He glanced at them, gave Jason an acknowledging nod then continued talking to his crew.

"Walk me through what happened," Jason said.

"It was a routine day," Ben said. "The cleanup crew was getting ready for the next extraction session and the surveying guys were checking the deposits." He pointed to the cave in the corner. "I was down there when I heard this loud sound. A couple of the lights and one of our catwalks crashed down, and unfortunately seven of our guys were injured." He shook his head. "Jones and Carrol are recovering in the infirmary, but the others had to be rushed to the hospital."

A grim thought entered his head. If those guys hadn't been shifters, they'd surely have been dead on impact. The look on Ben's face confirmed it. "What about their families?"

"We've contacted them. Probably on their way to the hospital now."

"Good. I'll make that my next stop." He scratched his chin. "Something doesn't feel right."

"You think?" Ben asked.

"Could be nothing," Jason said. "But my gut says otherwise."

"We'll tighten security. I haven't talked with our security company in a while. Dad and I had been telling Riva that we need our own crew instead of outsourcing it, but she kept putting off the decision."

"I'll talk to Matthew about it," Jason assured him. "Call me if you need anything else."

"Will do, cuz."

Jason followed the same path going outside the mine, his mind focused on the accident. He knew the mine operations inside and out, and how tightly controlled everything was. Safety was always a priority, even if all of their crew could survive life-threatening injuries. Was it a freak accident or something else?

As soon as he walked out of the cave, his phone started ringing. *Matthew*, he thought. And he was right.

"Did you find out anything yet?" his twin asked, the tension in his voice evident. Matthew was probably as edgy as he was. After all, they both considered everyone in Blackstone under their protection.

Jason relayed what Ben told him.

"And what do you think?" Matthew asked.

"It could be an accident."

"But…"

"I have a gut feeling."

Matthew let out a breath. "Me too. I don't know why."

"Maybe it's because we both know this is the first major accident in at least two generations," Jason said. "You know we always put the safety of our workers first."

"Right. What should we do?"

"Well, we'll have to keep an eye on things. What do you think about setting up our own security crew?"

"I'm sure we could swing it. I'll talk to our current contractors about a transition."

"Good. I'm on my way to the hospital, just to make sure our guys and their families are okay."

"Let me know if you want me to come by," Matthew said. "I'll make time."

"I will, but you focus on what you need to do. And your wedding," he added, hoping to have a lighthearted end to their conversation.

"Speaking of which … can you come to dinner tonight?"

"Dinner? Why?"

"Well, you know, Christina just arrived and we're having a welcome dinner. But no one else can make it, and I didn't want it to be awkward, just the three of us."

His dragon perked up. "What? Fuck, no." He probably sounded harsher than he wanted and his dragon agreed. "Besides, I've already seen her. Your lovely fiancé was called away on an emergency and I had to pick her up at the airport."

"Oh, really? I didn't know." Matthew's voice didn't sound convincing. "How was she?"

"Christina? Oh, she still hates me, don't worry," he huffed. "Which is why I probably shouldn't be there."

"C'mon, Jason. Please?"

"I've got plans."

"What other plans could you possibly have? Hanging out at The Den with Nathan?"

He let out a breath. "Fine." His inner dragon gave a contented snort. "I'll be there."

"Great. I'll see you later."

Jason frowned. He hoped he wouldn't regret this.

Jason was tired and hungry, but the last thing he wanted to do was battle his inner dragon and twin, so he drove right back to Blackstone Castle as soon as he was done. After he spent the afternoon with the families of the injured workers, he had to go straight back to his office at the Lennox Foundation to put out even more fires at work.

He was cranky and he hadn't eaten, and he told himself that he was only going back to Blackstone Castle so he could have one of Meg's fabulous dinners. Though he preferred living alone in his modern apartment in town, there was nothing like coming back to his childhood home and having a real meal.

Christopher, their butler, welcomed him home and informed him that everyone was in the dining room in the east wing. When he got there, Matthew, Catherine, and Christina were already seated. Catherine was in the middle of a story and Christina threw her head back and laughed. She looked gorgeous, with her blonde hair pinned up, and her blue, off-the-shoulder dress showing off her collarbones and an expanse of creamy skin. But it wasn't her outfit that made her beautiful. Rather, it was the genuine smile on her face, which promptly disappeared the moment her cool eyes landed on him.

"Nice of you to join us," Matthew said, raising a glass to him.

"How could I say no?" he said. Looking at the table, he saw that the empty place setting was right next to Christina. He sat down and flashed her a smile. "Did you get some rest?"

"I did, thank you," she said, taking a sip of her wine, her eyes carefully avoiding his.

"So," Matthew began. "Catherine was telling me about all the trouble she and Christina got into while they were in boarding school."

"All the trouble *she* got us into, you mean," Christina said wryly. "I only snuck out with her to make sure she didn't do anything too crazy."

Catherine giggled. "Oh c'mon, you had fun too." She turned to Matthew. "I know you're a stickler for rules, like my sister here, but don't tell me you've never had any wild stories from your youth?"

Matthew shook his head. "Wild stories are more of Jason's thing."

"Oh really?" Catherine asked. "Do tell."

"Well, there was that time during our senior trip in California…"

Jason groaned. "Don't." Normally, he didn't care about his reputation, but now wasn't the time for this particular story.

"What?" Matthew asked. "It wasn't that bad. Compared to all your other shenanigans later in life."

"So what happened?" Catherine asked.

"Basically, Jason came up with the idea of sneaking out and breaking into Disneyland after hours."

"No!" Catherine laughed. "Really?"

"Yes. He shifted, flew over the fence, and then turned off the security system."

"Did he get caught?" Christina asked.

"Oh yeah, the cameras caught him," Matthew said. "Mom and Dad swooped in and saved the day, of course. Grounded both of us for a month."

"Both of you?" Catherine exclaimed. "Why?"

"Because he wouldn't rat me out," Jason said. "They couldn't tell which one of us did it, though they both knew it was probably me."

"And why would you do that?" Catherine asked.

Matthew laughed. "Because Jason did it for me."

"He what?"

"I was the good kid, you know? Stayed at home to do homework. Straight A student." Matthew said. "Never did anything crazy or stupid. And I told him that it was the one thing I admired about him—not the stupid part, of course."

"Thanks," Jason said sarcastically.

"It was also the one thing I regretted. Not letting go and just being a kid. We were graduating that spring, after all." He gave Jason a warm smile. "And so Jason pretended to be me, snuck everyone into Disneyland, and basically everyone thought I was the coolest guy in school when we got back."

"Awww," Catherine said. "That's so sweet."

"You also scored with Jenny Davis on Space Mountain," Jason pointed out.

"It was 'It's a Small World' actually," Matthew corrected.

"Oh really?" Catherine asked, her brow raised.

"That was a long time ago, sweetheart." He gave her a kiss on the cheek. "Besides," he turned back to Jason. "I know what you did with Carmen Perez on the Jungle Cruise."

Jason laughed. "Touché."

The rest of the evening didn't turn out so badly. The food was excellent, as always. Meg had prepared roast lamb with rice and vegetables, plus bread pudding with ice cream for dessert. Matthew and Catherine kept the conversation going, and if they noticed that Christina and Jason weren't speaking to each other directly, they didn't say anything.

The thought irritated him. He was right beside her, but it was like he wasn't even there. His dragon must really be fucked up if this woman was supposed to be his mate. She was civil enough, but again, it was the indifference that was driving him crazy.

"Do you want to stay for a nightcap?" Matthew asked when they finished putting away the dishes. Meg, Christopher, and the rest of the staff had retired long ago, and so they had to clean up after themselves.

"Nah, I should head home."

"Okay, but let me walk you out." Matthew then turned to Christina and Catherine. "And you girls?"

"We have wedding stuff to do," Catherine said. "I need to go over a few things with Christina."

"All right, you go ahead then." He gave Catherine a quick kiss and then the girls left. "Did you find out anything else about the accident?" Matthew asked as they walked out of the east wing.

Jason shook his head. "No, nothing new. I can't talk to our guys yet, they were recovering when I got there. Maybe tomorrow."

"Keep me posted."

They reached the front door, but before Jason could open it, Matthew cleared his throat. "Wait."

"Yes?" he asked impatiently.

"There's one more thing we should talk about."

"What?"

"Christina."

"There's nothing to talk about," Jason said. "I should get going." But, as he opened the door, Matthew reached over his shoulder and slammed it shut. "What the hell?"

"Jason, we need to talk about this."

"About what, exactly?" he asked, crossing his arms over his chest.

"About what happened. And the fact that she can tell us apart."

"I told you, it was a fluke."

"Then why do you shut down every time we mention her name? And why has your dragon been difficult the past few weeks? Don't deny it."

"It's nothing," he said defensively.

"Look, if she's your mate—"

"She's not," he said flatly.

"But what if she is? Why are you denying yourself? Why would you deny her the chance to have a mate and share love—"

"First of all," Jason said, cutting him off. "This is none of your business. Second, in case you didn't notice, she hates me." And that truth cut him deep.

"She does not—"

"Will you let me finish? Lastly, I don't need a mate. I don't *want* a mate." He huffed. "My life is fine the way it is."

"Is it?" Matthew asked. "Running around screwing girls

left and right, spinning your wheels? Is that what you want the rest of your life?"

"For God's sake, are you going to turn into one of those married people? The one who thinks everyone should be paired off and pop out a bunch of kids and live happily ever after?"

"I don't mean to judge you," Matthew said. "Hell, you were the one who told me to go after Catherine, remember? I just thought, I've never been happier in my whole life, and that's all thanks to her. Is it wrong that I want that for you? My own brother?"

Jason sighed. "I am happy, the way I am. I don't want things to change."

Matthew shook his head in resignation. "Fine, I won't press it."

"Good." But Jason didn't feel any relief. In fact, the heaviness pressing on his chest grew. "I'll see you tomorrow. Goodnight, Matthew."

"Goodnight, Jason."

CHAPTER 4

"I REALLY DON'T SEE why we have to stay in Blackstone to go dress shopping," Christina said as they walked down Main Street. Catherine had driven them to the downtown area and parked a few blocks away from the wedding shop. "You know dad would have lent us the jet to go to Paris or London so you could have your trousseau. Mama would have wanted you to have the best."

"Chrissy," her sister said in an impatient voice. "This is a legit bridal shop, I swear. And the owner is really nice. She has all the latest gowns from New York and LA. Besides, I wanted you to meet the girls, and Sybil and Kate can't just take off a few days to go with us to Paris."

Christina snorted. "Fine."

"C'mon, we're already running late. And we still have to look over the flowers after this. If you'd have woken up on time—"

"I'm jet-lagged and tired," Christina whined. "Give me a break."

Irritation had been building in her since she arrived in

Blackstone. Aside from having another confrontation with Jason, Catherine was taking her sweet time. It turned out the wedding emergency that meant she couldn't pick her up from the airport was merely a case of the caterer throwing a fit over the lack of enoki mushrooms for the appetizers. When Catherine had finally arrived at Blackstone Castle two hours after Christina did, all she would talk about was Matthew and Blackstone, and all her new friends.

Christina knew that after being apart for a year, her sister would have changed, but she just hadn't realized how much. She wanted her sister back. She didn't want to feel resentful, but she wished it was like old times. Just her, Catherine, Cordy, their brothers, and Papa back home in Lykos.

"Catherine!" A petite older woman greeted when they entered The Foxy Bridal Boutique. "I'm glad you made it!"

"Sorry we're late, Angela," she said. "This is my sister, Christina."

"Nice to meet you," Angela said, extending her hand.

"Likewise." Christina took the other woman's hand gingerly. Maybe it was because she'd been around them all her life, but her instinct told her what the woman was. *Shifter.* Based on the cheeky little animal emblazoned on the boutique's sign, it was easy to guess what kind.

"Oh, you two are just gorgeous! Twins! And you're marrying a twin," Angela giggled then winked at Christina. "Care to make it a double wedding?"

"Er, no," she said coldly, ignoring the woman's puzzled look. "So, are we going to try on dresses or just stand here doing nothing?"

"Christina," Catherine hissed. "Sorry, Angela. She hasn't had her cup of coffee yet, hence the crankiness."

"That's quite all right," Angela said with a smile. "Your

friends are already inside the dressing room." She pointed toward the door on the other side of the main floor. "Go right ahead and I'll take out the dresses."

"Thank you."

Catherine tugged her toward the dressing room, and as soon as her sister opened the door, she knew this was a mistake. "Oh no. Them?" The two women waiting inside were very familiar.

Her sister gave her a puzzled look. "You've met Sybil and Kate?"

"You could say that." They were there the day she arrived at Blackstone Hospital and had her confrontation with Matthew. Apparently, they were all part of the conspiracy to get her away.

"Catherine!" One of the women hopped up from the couch, champagne glass in hand. "We started the party without you!" The bubble drink sloshed over the side of the glass, nearly spilling on Christina as the exuberant young woman hugged Catherine. "Where the hell have you been? Oh," she said when she looked at Christina. "Nice to see you. Again. Maybe we can be introduced this time."

"Chrissy," Catherine said. "This is Kate Caldwell."

"Hello, Kate." *Another shifter, of course.*

"Chrissy, good to meet you."

"Actually, only I get to call her Chrissy," Catherine laughed. "She hates it when anyone else shortens her name."

"Well, we can change that, can't we?" Kate asked, her green eyes twinkling. "After all, we've already plotted against her, poisoned her bodyguard, and now we're all going to be family."

"Please excuse my friend," the other woman interrupted as

she came over to them. "She thought it was a good idea to start on the champagne."

"At ten in the morning?" Christina asked.

"No better time!" Kate said as she grabbed the bottle from the bucket and topped off her glass.

The other young woman rolled her eyes then turned to Christina. "I'm Sybil."

Now that she had time for more than a fleeting glance, there was no mistaking who Sybil was related to. Silvery-gray eyes. Dark hair. That stubborn chin and full mouth. "You're Jason and Matthew's sister." Of course, she was a shifter as well. A rare female dragon.

She nodded. "Yup." Instead of offering her hand she hugged Christina. "It's nice to be introduced to you. And I'm really happy to be gaining not just one, but two sisters."

"Technically, only Catherine will be your sister-in-law," Kate pointed out.

"Technical, schmecnical," Sybil said. "It'll be awesome. More girls in the family. I'm so done with being outnumbered. And you have another sister, right?"

"Cordelia. Cordy," Catherine said. "She'll be here before the wedding, with Papa and our brothers."

"Awesome! Are your brothers hot?" Kate asked.

"Kate!"

A delicate throat clearing caught their attention. "Excuse me, ladies. I'm so sorry to rush, but I do have another appointment after you." Angela had come in with a rack of dresses. "I'll do my best to delay them."

"I'm really sorry, Angela," Catherine said. "We'll try to finish right away."

"You can always come in another day," Angela said. "I'll work day and night to have the dress finished in time."

"You don't have to, really. I'll find something today." Catherine walked over to the rack of dresses. "These are all beautiful. I don't know where to begin." She picked a dress off of the rack, something long with a delicately beaded belt. "What do you think?" she asked them.

"Try it on!" Kate urged. "C'mon, I didn't get up early for nothing!"

"Kate, you live five minutes from here," Sybil pointed out. "You were up at nine, tops."

"Meh." She took another sip of champagne. "On with the show."

Catherine disappeared into the back with Angela and the dress, while the rest of them sat down on the comfy couch.

"Champagne?" Kate offered.

"No, thank you," Christina said.

"More for me then," the younger woman said cheerfully.

Christina rolled her eyes. Sybil seemed nice enough, but this Kate ... she wasn't sure what to think of her. She was coarse, inappropriate, and too familiar. She couldn't believe that she had to share this special moment with these people. It should have been her, Cordy, and if she were alive, Mama, watching Catherine try on dresses for her big day.

"What do you think?"

Christina looked up, watching as her sister paraded the gown she'd selected. A lump caught in her throat. Catherine had never looked more beautiful, and it wasn't just the dress. Her face was glowing and her eyes sparkled. For the first time, she realized that yes, Catherine had changed—she was truly happy. She was free, not stifled as she had been back in Lykos. "Catherine ... you look ... "

"Perfect," Angela finished, beaming at them.

Christina nodded and sniffed. She stood up and walked

toward her sister. Catherine pulled her in for a hug. "I think … Mama would have … "

"I know," Catherine said, as she pulled away. There were tears forming in her eyes. "But you're here, with me. That's all that matters."

Shame filled her, and Christina realized how selfish she'd been. She should be happy that Catherine had finally found a place where she belonged, with someone she loved. Matthew Lennox really was a good man and she knew her sister would always be loved and safe with him.

Angela handed them a tissue. "Don't worry, ladies, I'm always prepared."

Everyone burst into laughter, and Christina accepted the tissue gratefully and wiped her eyes.

"Ugh, c'mon," Kate said. "Enough with this sentimental crap! We want more dresses! More dresses! More dresses!"

Sybil rolled her eyes and took the champagne glass away from Kate. "That's enough. Time to sober up, Kate."

The other woman pouted and sank down onto the couch. "You're such a wet blanket."

Catherine tried on several more gowns. Indeed, Angela had outdone herself. All the wedding gowns looked gorgeous on her.

"I just can't decide," she said as she tried on the last gown. "Should I try on my favorite ones again?"

"No, wait!" Kate said. "I have a better idea. You need to be able to see what you look like from other people's perspective."

"And how is she supposed to do that?" Sybil asked.

"Duh," Kate jerked a thumb at Christina. "Catherine has a real live look-alike mannequin."

"Huh?" Sybil asked.

"That's a great idea!" Catherine clapped her hands together. "Chrissy, you try on the gowns and then I can see how it looks on me."

Christina's eyes widened. "No way. I'm not trying on wedding gowns!"

"Please, Chrissy?"

"Yes," Kate said. "Please, Chrissy?"

Christina looked at Angela. "Surely you have some store policy against that?"

The fox shifter shook her head. "Not at all. I think it's a great idea."

"Yay!" Kate stood up and grabbed one of the dresses. "Let's go, Chrissy."

Christina had trained during the past year to be a field agent, working out and even going to boot camp for a month with other recruits. Her brothers had also taught her self-defense and martial arts for years before that. Still, she was no match for Kate's brute strength and sheer determination, and found herself being dragged into the back of the dressing room.

"What are you—hey!"

Kate was unbuttoning the front of her blouse. "You're not shy, are you? Don't worry, I don't play for the other team. Though I have to admit, your tits are pretty hot."

"What? Stop it!" But Kate was relentless and had already made quick work of her blouse. "Fine! Just let me do it," she grumbled. There was no way she was getting out of this, so she quickly undressed and put on the gown. It was the third one Catherine had tried. The top was made entirely of lace with a sweetheart neckline and puffy ball gown skirt with a long train.

"Ah, good, good," Kate said, fiddling her fingers together. "Excellent. Let's go show the girls."

She followed Kate outside and then stood on the small dais. "Well?" she asked the other women.

"This was a great idea," Sybil said. "What do you think, Catherine?"

"Hmmm…" Catherine tapped her finger on her chin. "You know, I really liked wearing this one and I thought it looked good on me. But now that I think about it, it seems like something you would wear, Chrissy."

"Excuse me?" she asked. "We're shopping for you, remember?"

"I know," her sister said. "But, you've always been the more traditional one, I think. I feel like this is the gown you'd pick if *you* were getting married."

Christina looked at herself in the mirror. *Hmmm.* Catherine knew her well. A little too well. It was something a princess would wear and she had been the more girly of the two of them growing up.

"Excuse me, ladies, I hate to intrude, but are you…"

Christina turned around at the sound of the familiar voice, the voluminous skirts whipping around her. "What are you doing here?"

Jason stared up, his eyes darkening as his gaze raked over her in the white gown. Heat crept up her neck and suddenly the dress felt too tight and the room too small.

"You can't see your bride in her gown before the wedding day!" Kate shrieked as she lunged in front of Christina.

Jason shook his head. "I'm not Matthew."

"And she's not me," Catherine said, getting to her feet. "What are you doing here, Jason?"

"Matthew's waiting outside. He wanted to surprise you

and take you girls to lunch," he explained. "He didn't want to accidentally see the gown, so he sent me to check on you."

"Aww, that's sweet," Sybil said.

"We're not done yet," Catherine said. "Could you guys wait a little longer?

"Sure," he said with a shrug.

Christina stared after him, watching his retreating back as he left without even giving her a second glance. She still couldn't believe he saw her in a wedding gown, of all things.

"Chrissy?" Catherine asked, waving her hand in front of her face. "Are you okay?"

"Huh? Uh, yeah, I'm fine." She cleared her head and gave her sister a weak smile. "So, which one should I try next?"

CHAPTER 5

"ARE THEY DONE YET?" Matthew asked as Jason walked past him.

"No." *But I am,* he added silently as he walked away.

The cold air felt good as it hit his face. The wind wasn't biting anymore, and to him, it felt more like a cool breeze. He kept walking down Main Street with no real destination in mind.

Surely that wasn't something Matthew planned. His brother's words from last night had struck something in him and he couldn't stop thinking about it. *Mate.* It was ringing in his head over and over again. And now, seeing Christina wearing a wedding dress...

"What's the matter with you?" Matthew asked as he caught up to him.

"Nothing."

"C'mon, just talk to me."

"I said nothing, okay?" He really wasn't up for another discussion. "Look, something came up."

"At the mines?" Matthew asked, his expression changing. "Did you get new information?"

"Maybe, not sure." He didn't want to lie to Matthew, so he thought of an excuse. "I should go to the hospital and check on our guys. See if the families need help." It wasn't a lie and it was his job to take care of them.

"Of course. Just keep me updated."

"Will do."

With one last nod, Matthew walked away.

Finally alone, Jason thought about his options. He could wait it out. Christina would be gone in less than a week, but he wasn't sure he could control his dragon for that long, and it would be difficult to avoid her. So what was he supposed to do?

He needed a distraction. There was that hot brunette from the The Den last week. She came to Blackstone for a girls' weekend, he remembered that Nate hooked up with one of her friends. Julie? No, Jessica. She was getting cozy, but his dragon wouldn't let him seal the deal. *Asshole.*

He pulled his phone from his pocket and scrolled down, then found her name. His finger hovered over the screen for a few seconds before he dialed.

"Hello?"

"Hello, Jessica? This is Jason. Lennox. We met at The Den in Blackstone last week."

"Oh," she said in a breathy voice. "I was beginning to think you were never going to call me."

He could almost see her pout. "Yeah, well, I had some work stuff come up. I was wondering, are you free?"

"Free? When?"

"I was thinking tonight … "

CHAPTER 6

"You made the right choice," Angela said as she handed Catherine her credit card. "You're going to be gorgeous, and I won't have to make too many adjustments."

"Thanks, Angela," she said. "You've been great. Especially considering how last minute everything is."

"I really appreciate you helping," Matthew added.

"No worries at all," the other woman replied, her eyes warm. "Now, don't stress, okay? Just enjoy your day. Both of you."

"I will!" Catherine waved goodbye to Angela as they left the shop.

Matthew had been waiting for them in the boutique, safely outside the dressing area. There was no sign of Jason, but Matthew told them that he had to deal with things at work and wouldn't be joining them for lunch. Christina wasn't sure if she was relieved or disappointed.

Matthew took them to lunch at Rosie's Bakery and Cafe. He explained Rosie had been there almost forever, and a place where he and his family would frequent when he was growing up. After lunch, Matthew left them because he had to run back to the office and they had more wedding errands to run.

"Where to?" Christina asked.

"Flower shop, then the cake shop. Oh, we should swing by the jewelry store as well. I know we didn't have time to get you all the same dresses, but you should at least have some matching accessories."

As the day progressed, Christina actually found herself enjoying the company of the other two girls, despite her initial reservations. Kate was certainly an acquired taste, but she found the younger woman's crude sense of humor amusing. She had taken an immediate liking to Sybil, though it was probably because she reminded her of Cordy in some ways— the peacemaker and always the one to make sure everyone was comfortable and having a good time. She was also surprised that Sybil worked as a social worker, especially considering the vast wealth and privilege she had grown up with.

It was already late so they all decided to have dinner at one of the restaurants in town. After their meal, the four women walked out in good spirits.

"Thanks so much for taking the day off to go shopping with me," Catherine said. "I had so much fun."

"And the night isn't over yet," Kate said.

"What do you mean?" Christina asked.

"Oh no, what did you do?" Sybil exclaimed. "Kate … "

"Well—"

She was interrupted by a loud horn that played an obnoxious tune. Three heads whipped around, their faces in varying degrees of surprise, shock, and horror at the gigantic pink Hummer limo that pulled up in front of them.

"Surprise!" Kate waved her arms in the air. "This is your bachelorette party."

"What?" Catherine's face went pale. "You didn't!"

"I did."

"I told you I didn't want a bachelorette party," Catherine said.

"And I said you were getting one, so here we are." Kate grabbed the door handle and pulled it open. "What? There aren't any half naked men hiding in there. I like my hide un-burnt, thank you very much."

"Where are you taking us?" Sybil asked.

"We're just going to The Den," Kate explained as she scrambled up into the limo. "I got this for us so we don't have to drive or ask anyone else to bring us home."

Sybil crossed her arms over her chest. "And how much are you planning to drink?"

"Let's just say, if you can't find me by the morning of the wedding, you better send out an APB."

Catherine explained to Christina that The Den was a local bar, and the place she worked as a bartender when she first came to Blackstone.

"Tim's a great boss," her sister said. "If a little gruff."

The Den was lively for a weekday night, but then again, it was one of the few bars in town. As soon as they entered, they were greeted by a petite, curvy redheaded waitress.

"You're new," Catherine said. "I mean, you weren't here when I was the bartender."

The waitress shook her head and gave her a shy smile. "Yeah, I just started a few weeks ago. My first night working was your engagement party, actually. My name's Penny. Tim has your table all ready. He asked that I take good care of you."

Penny led them to a table in the corner, which had been decorated with pink feather boas, glitter confetti, balloons, and penis-shaped banners.

"I picked out all the decor," Kate said proudly.

Sybil flashed Kate a dirty look as she gingerly pushed the paper phalluses aside so she could sit down. "Really? I couldn't tell."

"Penny, my girl!" Kate said. "Four shots of tequila, please. Now," she said to her companions. "What will you be having?"

Despite her reservations, Christina found herself having an even better time. She had drunk three glasses of wine and was feeling a little tipsy. Catherine seemed to be enjoying herself, and introduced more of her former work friends as they came by to offer their congratulations. All of them seemed genuine enough, except for maybe one or two, though Christina had a sneaking suspicion it was because of jealousy. After all, Catherine had landed the most eligible bachelor in town.

"A toast to the bride-to-be," Kate said, raising her shot glass. Christina had lost count of how much the other woman had drank, but then again Kate was a shifter and could drink any human under the table without batting an eyelash. "I wish you happiness, love and … who am I kidding? Hot sex, orgasms, and tons of little dragonlings are all you need for a happy life." She knocked back a shot of tequila.

"I won't even try to beat that," Christina said. "You win."

Kate threw her head back and laughed. "You know? I thought you were kind of a bitch when we first met, but now, I like you." She offered her a shot. "Here, this'll help you relax."

"No, but thanks," she said. "I'll stick to wine."

"Spoilsport."

"Hello, ladies, I didn't know you were having a party." A man had walked up behind Kate and Sybil, and put his arms around their chairs. Christina narrowed her eyes at him. He was handsome, in that devil-may-care kind of way, with his long, sandy-blond hair and mischievous green eyes. Like most shifters, he was tall and looked like he worked out every day of the year. He also looked very familiar.

"Yeah, that's because you weren't invited, moron," Kate said, rolling her eyes.

"Chrissy," Catherine began. "This is Nate, Kate's brother."

"By blood only," Kate drolled.

Ah, that's why. Nate looked like a masculine version of Kate. Friendly green eyes turned to her. "Nice to meet... whoah...sorry. Seeing you both side-by-side is a little mind-boggling."

"Aren't you going to hit on her, too?" Kate asked.

He shook his head. "Uh, no. No offense," he said to Christina. "But it's a little weird. With you two being twins and all."

"And the fact that I must have turned you down ten times," Catherine added.

"Six times," Nathan corrected with a grin. "But, I'm not disappointed you didn't fall for my charms. You can't stop fate, right? With you and Matthew being mates and all."

Catherine laughed. "I guess not."

Nathan sidled up to Christine. "So, are you single?" he asked, flashing her a smile.

"I'm afraid so," Christina answered, taking a sip of her wine. "I thought you said you weren't interested in me?"

"I said I thought it was weird," he corrected. "But I could probably get over it."

Nathan was charming and hot, she had to give him that. But still, no matter how hard she tried, she couldn't muster anything more than friendly interest in him. Yet, when it came to someone else...

"Christina is a nice girl," Sybil said. "So stay away from her."

"Jeez, can't a guy have some fun?"

"Someday, Nathan Caldwell, when you meet your mate, I hope she makes you chase after her," Sybil said.

Nathan snorted. "I told you before, I'm never getting a mate or getting married. Matthew and Catherine being an exception, all that love and mating shit is for losers." He turned his head toward the front door. "*Finally.* I was wondering when he'd get here."

"Who?" Sybil turned around. "Ah, your partner in crime, my brother."

"Sorry, Nate," Kate said as she glanced toward the door. "Looks like he's not alone."

Christina felt a knot slowly begin to grow in her stomach as she followed Kate's gaze. Jason indeed wasn't alone. A gorgeous brunette was clinging to him, and his arm was around her waist. She gripped the edge of the table, her fingernails digging into the wood. Catherine sent her a strange look.

"You know, Jason usually leaves with a girl at the end of the night," Kate said. "He's never walked in with one at the start. Who is she?" Kate looked at her brother. "Do you know her?"

Nate shook his head. "Never seen her before, though she does look familiar. I think she's been here before. Jason might have talked to her." His eyes lit up. "Ah, she was on a girl's night last weekend. In fact, I brought one of her friends back to my place."

"Eww, TMI," Sybil said. "But, Jason seeing a girl for a second time? Doesn't seem like his style."

An uncomfortable sensation crept up Christina's spine and made her chest feel tight. She tried to pry her gaze away from Jason and the woman, but she couldn't turn away. They walked over to the bar and he signaled to the bartender. The brunette draped herself around him and whispered something into his ear. Christina felt the air squeeze out of her lungs.

"Are you okay, Chrissy?" Catherine asked. "Want to go to the ladies room?"

"I'm fine." Catherine grabbed her wine glass and drained it. "You go ahead."

"Are you—"

"I said I'm fine." She looked at Kate and nodded at her shot glasses. "Is the offer still open?"

Kate whooped. "That's my girl!" She slid over one of the glasses toward her. Christina immediately picked it up and drank it. "Yeah!" She signaled to Penny, who ran over to refill the four shot glasses.

Catherine cleared her throat. "If you'll excuse me," she said, grabbing her purse. "I need to take a little trip to the ladies' room."

As Catherine walked away, Christina took one last glance toward Jason. Big mistake. Jason was now nuzzling the brunette's neck. She quickly turned away, the sudden motion making her dizzy.

"Do you think that girl is Jason's mate?" Sybil asked.

Nate snorted. "No way. Jason doesn't do mates or that love shit either."

"Still, it would be nice if he could settle down, like Matthew with Catherine," Sybil said. "A mate. Not only one his dragon recognizes, but one that the Sinclair legend validates. Dragon mate *and* soul mate."

"What legend?" Christina asked.

"Oh, Catherine never told you?"

She shook her head.

"Well, you know shifters have mates, right?"

Christina nodded. "My adoptive father is a wolf shifter and my mother was his mate." Being human, she didn't understand all of that. Papa had explained that it was like being in love with someone, but much, much bigger and deeper. That's why it had nearly driven him mad when she died.

"Well, my mother is a human and she had this saying in her family: the one who knows you from your twin is your soul mate."

"But what does it mean?" Christina asked.

"We thought it was a joke, growing up," Sybil said. "But apparently, it's true with Matthew and Catherine."

"What's true?"

"That Catherine can tell Matthew and Jason apart."

Pressure began to build behind Christina's eyes. "W-what?"

"Apparently to her, Matthew and Jason look different, which is weird, right? Even Mom can't tell them apart."

"Right." She reached for one of Kate's shot glasses and knocked back the tequila. The burn felt good. At least she knew that the feeling was coming back to her body, based on the path the liquid burned down her throat. She took a deep breath then took another shot.

The tequila had helped push back that dreaded pit in her stomach but it was slowly creeping back. *This was crazy.*

Insane. Catherine definitely knew *she* could tell Jason and Matthew apart, too. Did her sister realize...? Of course she did. And she had kept quiet this whole time.

No, it couldn't be. She was no mate, not to anyone, and certainly not to Jason Lennox.

"Uhm, Christina?" Kate said. "I'm all for having fun, but that's gonna be your fourth shot. Slow down, yeah?"

Christina stared at the clear liquid in the shot glass in her hand before gulping down every single drop. "Now I'm done," she said, slamming the glass down. "I think I need some air."

She whipped around, making sure she wasn't looking toward Jason and his date as she made her way out. She thought she heard Catherine's voice calling her, but she ignored it and made her way out of the building.

The cold evening air washed over her, and for a moment, her mind cleared. Obviously Catherine knew. Why would her sister keep something like that from her? And Jason ... did he suspect?

Maybe Catherine knew about his reputation and didn't want her hurt. Nathan said Jason didn't do the mate thing.

Her knees felt weak and she braced herself against the door. Except for that time in the car, he'd been flirty, but he'd never said anything. In fact, he'd downright ignored her at dinner last night. It had irritated her, but she hadn't let it show.

She calmed herself. Maybe it wasn't true. Surely, someone else could tell Jason and Matthew apart? Besides if they were mates, Jason's dragon would have known. He obviously didn't want her.

The faint sound of voices knocked her out of her reverie. She couldn't make out what they were saying, but there was something that didn't feel right. And she trusted her instinct.

She walked around the building toward the back, to what she assumed was the employees entrance. Looking around the corner, she stopped and tried to listen in case she was wrong.

"Please, I have to get back to work..."

"Aww, c'mon. Just hang out with me for a bit. I'm sure your boss won't mind. I'm a good customer."

"But—"

"I'm sure he'd be disappointed if you didn't stay and keep me company."

"Well ... no, please! Don't touch me!" A scream rang out.

Christina seethed with mounting rage and without another thought she marched toward the two voices. A large shadowy figure loomed over a small one. Without hesitation, she grabbed him by the shoulder and pulled him away.

"What the fuck!" The figure staggered back and the stink of alcohol assaulted her senses. The large man swung around, his face red under the lamplight. "Hey, mind your own business, bitch!" He lunged at her.

Christina's lips curled into a smile. *Finally*.

CHAPTER 7

"JASON, did you hear what I said?"

"Huh? What?" Jason's head snapped back toward Jessica. "Sorry, babe, I was, uh, distracted by work stuff."

Jessica's full, red lips turned out into a pout. "I drove all the way here and got dressed up for you, and you're thinking about work?"

"Aww, sorry," he said, leaning in close. Her perfume was sticky and cloying, but he forced himself to nuzzle at her neck. "Won't happen again."

"Good."

He searched his brain, trying to figure out what she had been saying. Since they met at the restaurant where they had dinner, she'd been talking about herself—where she got her hair done, her nails, her expensive clothes, and her boring job. "So, tell me again about your evil boss?"

"Oh, yeah. Well the other day, I'm like, texting with my friend Gina—she's like, in crisis mode because she caught her boyfriend in bed with some skank, right? Anyway, he catches me texting her and it's like, almost my break, yeah? And then..."

Jason pasted another smile on his face and nodded. Pretending to listen to chicks was a skill he'd perfected over the years. But he wasn't zoning out right now as Jessica continued to talk about her boss. No, his mind and gaze kept wandering over the table across the room.

Motherfucker. He didn't know Catherine was having her bachelorette party tonight. Of course, he didn't think to ask, but still ... the moment he walked in and saw Christina, he knew this was a mistake. Correction: the moment he saw Jessica at the restaurant, he knew it was a mistake. His damn dragon knew this was wrong and was making him pay.

It was a good thing Jessica was human or she'd have felt the fight the animal inside him was putting up. But he carried on with the farce of a date anyway as he didn't want to humiliate Jessica by simply telling her the date was over. He may be a bastard when it came to women, but he wasn't a *heartless* bastard.

He should have ended the date right after dinner, but she'd insisted on coming here. Did Christina see them yet? Didn't seem like it. She was casually chatting and sipping on her wine without a care in the world. Then she started flirting with Nate...

He loved Nate like a brother, but he was well aware of what his friend was thinking. As soon as he cozied up to Christina, Jason knew what he was doing. He'd have done the same thing after all, and knowing how hard he pursued Catherine, he knew Nate would be relentless. He kept his gaze fixed on them, his body tensing as the seconds ticked by.

He shook his head. This was getting to be too much. Maybe he should just turn his attention back on his date.

"Jason!" Jessica snapped. "Now what's the matter?"

"Huh? I'm listening, babe."

"Good," she said with a smug smile. "So, that's a yes then? On my last question?"

"Yeah, sure, whatever."

He glanced back at the table and frowned. Christina was gone. Where the hell was she? Catherine had come back from the bathroom, Kate was slamming back more tequilas while Sybil watched, and Nate ... well, he was gone too.

"Bastard," he growled and disentangled Jessica's arms from his torso. He didn't even give a backward glance as he marched toward the door. He pushed it open, storming out into the dark parking lot. He recognized Nate's figure, standing in front of the doorway, scratching his head.

"Where is she?" He grabbed him by the shoulders and spun him around.

Nate's eyes glowed an eerie green and a growl escaped his throat, the wolf inside him making its presence known. But when he saw Jason, he reared back. "What the fuck, man?" His eyes, returning to normal, looked confused. "Who are you talking about?"

"Christina," he said through gritted teeth. "Where is she?"

"I don't know!" He put his hands up. "Catherine asked me to check on her. But she's gone."

A cry and then a moan from somewhere in the back of the building caught their attention, making them both start. His dragon roared and he sprang into action, reaching the source of the sound within seconds.

A man was lying prone on the ground. Standing over him was Christina, looking down at him with disgust on her face. A fierce determination marred her features, but as she looked up, her face softened. "Jason?"

"Christina." He approached her slowly. "What happened?"

She shrugged. "He slipped. And fell. Then hit his head and knocked himself out."

Something wasn't right, he could feel it. "Should we call for an ambulance?"

She glanced over to her side. Jason didn't notice the other woman pressed up against the side of the building, sheer terror in her wide, green eyes. "You okay, Penny?" she asked.

The young woman's pretty face was ashen, but she nodded.

"Did he touch you?"

Penny shook her head, but her whole body was trembling.

Christina squatted down and leaned over the man, checked his pulse, and then his head. "He's not bleeding out. I'm sure he'll live," she said, pure distaste dripping from her voice. "You could wait a bit until he regains consciousness. I'm going to go back to the girls."

He watched as Christina casually walked away without a second glance. *What the hell happened?* Jason turned to Penny, but the young waitress scampered away before he could say anything. He told Nate to take the guy to Blackstone Hospital, and his friend simply carried the unconscious man over his shoulder and loaded him into his car.

He was still puzzled. It didn't look like the guy had any injuries from the fall. Maybe a small bump on the back of his head, but nothing that would knock him out. The man was over six feet tall and probably 250 pounds, though most of it was fat around his middle. There was something else going on.

Jason walked back into The Den, intending to find out the truth. There was no sign of Penny. Or Jessica, for that matter. But, Christina was definitely there. In fact, she was the center of attention. A group had formed around the girls' table, laughing and cheering.

"Slam it down, girl!" Kate hooted. "C'mon!" She filled another shot glass in Christina's hand from the bottle. "One more! One more! One more!"

"Excuse me," Jason said as he pushed his way into the crowd. He grabbed the glass.

"Hey!" Christina slurred. "I wasn't done with that."

"Oh, you're done," he said, tossing the glass aside. He grabbed her hand. "C'mon, time to go home."

"I'm said I'm not—stop! Put me down!"

"*Holy shitballs!*" someone, probably Kate said.

Christina weighed nothing at all, and he patted her backside as he slung her over his shoulder. "Party's over," he said to the other girls. "Get in your party bus and go home."

"Let me go, you...brute! *Vlaca!*" He strongly suspected it wasn't a very complimentary word, directed as it was with pure venom toward his backside. She let out a string of curses in a foreign language, but he ignored her.

"Where are you taking her?" Catherine shouted. "Are you bringing her back to the castle?"

"I'm gonna sober her up first." He continued walking outside, Christina screeching like a banshee.

"I said put me down!" She beat her fists on his back. "Where are you taking me?"

"We're gonna get some hot coffee and then you're going to tell me what happened tonight." They were a few feet away from his truck and all he had to do was open the door and push her inside.

"I can't ... Oh my God, everything's going black..." She went limp in his arms.

"*Mother*—" He gritted his teeth and then eased her down,

setting her on her feet, his hands holding her steady. Her eyes were closed and her head lolled back. "*Christina*. Are you okay? Wake up!"

Her eyes flew open and then she moved away from him, quick as a rabbit. Jason let out a curse. Still, she was no match for his speed and she only got a few steps away before he caught up with her.

"Bloody hell," she shrieked. He pulled her back to his truck, pinning her against the side. "Let me go! Why are you doing this?"

"Why am I doing this?" he roared. "Dammit—" He couldn't stop himself even if he wanted to, and his mouth came crashing down on hers.

She struggled for a moment, a snarl escaping her lips, but he silenced her and soon she was returning his kiss. Eager, wet, and warm. She tasted like sunshine, like berries bursting with ripeness.

Arms snaked around his middle, pulling him closer. He obliged, pressing her up against the truck, letting her feel how much he wanted her. A gasp escaped her mouth as his rock-hard cock pressed against her stomach. He'd been hard the moment their lips touched. Hell, he'd been sporting this hard-on for her since they met.

Moving his lips lower, he nuzzled at her neck, her sweet scent wrapping around him. "Jason," she moaned, pushing her body up against him. He hooked his hand under her thigh and wrapped her leg around his waist. She arched her back and ground her hips over his erection.

He could come right now, dry-humping her against the side of his truck. But that wouldn't sate him at all. He knew he had to have her, be inside her.

He slipped his hands down her back and then inside her

leggings, over the sweet curves of her ass and between her cheeks. His fingers skimmed lightly over her tight little rear hole and she shivered. *Maybe another time*, he thought, as his digits found what he wanted. She was already wet, her pussy lips dripping.

"Fuck, baby, you're incredible." This was better than in his imagination.

"Jason, please."

Did she even know what she was begging for? From the wetness on his fingers, he knew. He pushed a finger inside her tentatively, making her tense, and then relax against him.

"More," she rasped. "More."

Blood roared in his ears and he captured her lips again, his tongue dipping into her mouth as his fingers did the same to her tight little snatch.

She cried into his mouth, and he felt her tighten. She threw her head back, banging it against the glass, and let out a desperate yelp. He thrust deep into her, her slick cunt gripping his fingers as she came, her body shuddering then slumping against him. Withdrawing his hands from her, he lifted his fingers to his mouth and tasted her.

God, she was fucking amazing. This felt amazing. It felt *right*.

"Christina," he whispered against her neck.

"Jason, I…" Her body froze. "Jason, this isn't…" She placed her hands on his chest and pushed him gently away.

Confusion muddled his brain. "What's going on?"

"I just—" She shook her head. "Why did you kiss me?"

"I did more than kiss you," he said.

"We can't do this."

Her words washed over him like cold water. "What do you mean?"

"It's just that…you…" She stammered. "You don't really want this, do you? I'm just convenient, the closest girl you can get your hands on."

Irritation scratched at him. "What the hell are you talking about?"

"What about her?"

"Who?"

Anger burned in her eyes. "That *girl* you were with?"

Shit. Jessica. He'd forgotten about her. "She was nothing."

She let out a sarcastic laugh. "Which just proves my point."

"Excuse me?" What the hell was she going on about?

"I know your type," she spat. "You jump from one bed to another—"

"Stop!"

"Well, do you deny it?"

He couldn't of course. And how dare she, anyway? He was single and free and he never hurt anyone, at least not on purpose. Whenever he took a girl home, he made his intentions clear: one night only. He never pretended to be anyone else and didn't need to apologize for being who he was. But, the look in her eyes … was she hurt? His own emotions were making it too hard to judge. "I'll take you back."

"No," she said. "The girls are still here." She nodded to the pink Hummer across the parking lot. "I'll get a ride with them."

He watched her go, his feet rooted to the spot.

Mine!

"For the last time, shut the fuck up!" He was done. Done with this whole thing. He was going to ignore his dragon from now on. If the pain ripping in his chest was any indication, mates were much more trouble than they were worth.

CHAPTER 8

CHRISTINA'S HEAD throbbed and she let out a groan as she pulled the covers over her head. It was too bright and the sun was shining even behind her closed eyelids. Peeking from under the covers, she realized the curtains had been left open and the sunshine was streaming through the windows.

She groaned and pulled the covers down. *What happened?* She looked around, her brain still muddled with sleep, though the pain splitting her skull reminded her. Alcohol. Too much of it. And—

"Glad you're awake, Sleeping Beauty."

She whipped toward the sound of the voice, covering her eyes as the blades of sunlight seemed to penetrate her head. "Ugh ... Catherine? Did you stay here all night?"

"I almost did," she said. She was sitting on the couch in the sitting area, a magazine on her lap. "But Matthew dragged me back to bed. I came by a couple of minutes ago to make sure you were okay."

"Yeah, I guess I'm okay." Catherine stood up and walked over to her, then handed her a bottle of water and two pills.

"Thanks," she said accepting them gratefully. She washed down the pills with water. "Uhm, how did I get here?"

"You don't remember?" Catherine asked in an incredulous voice.

"Uh, some of it." *Only up to the part where I almost had sex with Jason Lennox.* She groaned and fell back onto the bed. Did that really happen? Her body was screaming yes. And screaming for another earth-shattering orgasm.

But, it was too much. The desire burning in her, the emotional maelstrom he was putting her through. She wanted him, but at the same time, she couldn't be his mate. It just couldn't be true. She had a life, she had a job. There were so many people out there depending on her and there was still one more thing she had to do. *Avenge Mama.*

Being here had already distracted her so much and took her away from her work. In the last three days since she had been here, she hadn't even checked her phone or email. The other agents might have put in more intelligence on the smuggling ring and who was behind them. And she wanted to get back into the field. Beating up that man who tried to molest Penny last night had been satisfying on some level. She hated people who thought they could do anything they want, just because they were bigger and stronger.

This whole mate thing was all a distraction. Jason Lennox was a distraction. Besides, all he wanted was a quick lay. She'd have gladly given in except that the things he made her feel ... they scared her.

"Hello—Earth to Christina," Catherine said, interrupting her thoughts. "You feeling better?"

"Mildly." The medicine seemed to be working because she was starting to think clearer and managed to put the whole mate thing aside.

"A shower should help. Go and get ready," Catherine urged. "Matthew arranged a surprise for us."

"Ugh, can't I stay in bed?"

Her sister pointed to the bathroom. "Go."

She trudged to the shower, muttering under her breath. However, she had to admit, Catherine was right. The shower made her feel better.

"Ready?" Catherine asked when she exited the bathroom, dressed in her jeans, socks, and sweater dress.

"Where are we going?" she asked as she ran a brush through her hair.

"You'll see."

As Catherine drove them further and deeper up the mountains, Christina had to admit it was beautiful. She'd even seen a few animals on the way up—some deer, raccoons, and rabbits. After nearly an hour of driving, they got off the main road and drove through the gates of a fenced-in area, then parked in the middle of a group of trailers.

"Where are we?" Christina asked as they walked up to the mouth of a very large cavern.

"Matthew arranged a tour of the blackstone mines for us," Catherine explained. She checked in with the security booth at the mouth of the cave, then handed Christina a vest and hard hat.

"The mines?" She knew that one of Lennox Corporation's main products was blackstone, the hardest substance on earth. It made sense that Matthew would want to show off their greatest asset, though it was an unusual way to spend the morning.

"Yeah, they're extracting today, so he wanted us to see it."

Christina shrugged. At least the cave was dark and helped her headache. *Ugh, damn Kate and her tequila.*

Halfway into the cave, they were met by a tall, broad-shouldered man carrying a clipboard and wearing the same safety gear as them.

"Ben!" Catherine greeted as she waved to him.

"Hey, Catherine." The handsome, bearded man returned her smile. "How's the wedding planning?"

"Good, good. This is my sister, Christina. Christina, this is Ben Walker, Matthew's cousin."

"Hey, Christina," Ben greeted. "Nice to meet ya."

"Likewise," she said. As she returned Ben's firm handshake, she knew he was also a shifter. Well, he was related to the Lennoxes. But he didn't seem like a dragon.

"C'mon," he nodded toward one of the caves. "Let's hurry or you'll miss the show."

"Show?" Neither Ben nor Catherine answered her, so she followed them. LED string lights led the way, but it was still too dark. The shifters in here probably didn't even need them, but her human eyes were weak, so she held onto Catherine's hand as they trudged along the dark and damp cavern. She could see the light at the end, and by the time they reached the next cavern, she was squinting, trying to adjust her vision.

"Okay, we're here," Ben said.

As her eyes adjusted to the light, she saw that the space inside was huge. The ceilings were probably over fifty feet high, and the width twice that.

Despite the open space, there was something that filled the air. Anticipation. The lights flickered off, plunging them into darkness. And when the ground rumbled, Christina grabbed her sister's shoulders. "What's going on?"

"Wait."

Suddenly, the cavern was filled with a hot, bright light. The temperature must have soared to over a hundred degrees and she turned away from the brightness. Someone—Ben, maybe—handed her a pair of safety glasses and she put them on.

A gasp escaped her lips. A gigantic dragon was standing in the middle of the cave, breathing fire at the walls. Gold scales covered its body like armor, its massive wings stretched out. It spewed fire for a good minute before stopping, plunging the cave into darkness. It paused then started the cycle over again.

The dragon did this a few more times and when it finally stopped, overhead lights flickered on. A few seconds later, workers began to scramble forward to dig through the piles of rubble left behind.

"Amazing," Catherine said.

"You've never seen it before?" Christina asked.

She shook her head. "No, I never had the time. Matthew's only told me about how they mine the blackstone. This mountain has the only deposit in the world, and they've been mining it for generations."

"Huh." Interesting. She had no idea. No wonder the Lennoxes were so powerful and rich.

The dragon had stepped back from the commotion, folding in its wings to make way for the workers. It began to shrink, slowly, getting smaller and smaller.

"So, aside from being CEO, Matthew has to come here and do this?"

"Sometimes. It's good for dragons too, apparently, to let some of their fire out every now and then," Ben explained. "But that's not Matthew."

Oh no. That meant…

The naked, fully human figure was down on one knee. Christina could see the rise and fall of Jason's broad shoulders as he breathed deeply. Her eyes trailed down his muscled, sweaty back, down to the curve of his taut backside. Catherine politely turned away, and she followed suit, despite the fact that she wanted to keep staring at his naked body. She was glad for the darkness of the cave as it hid the redness in her cheeks as she remembered what happened during the bachelorette party.

One of the workers handed Jason a set of clothes and he got dressed, apparently oblivious to their presence. He walked over to the other workers, chatting with them casually.

"Let's go say hi," Catherine said.

Christina hesitated, not really wanting to talk to Jason right now, not after last night. But it wasn't like she had a choice. Her sister would know something had happened if she refused. She straightened her spine. They were adults here. Surely they could all act like it.

"Jason," Ben called. "We have visitors."

Jason turned around quickly. "Visitors? Who?"

Christina's body went rigid when their eyes met and a coldness swept over her.

His mouth set into a hard line and his jaw tensed. "Oh, hello, Catherine. Christina." He gave them a curt nod. "Did you come here for a tour?"

"Yes," Catherine answered. "Didn't Matthew tell you?"

"No."

"He must have forgotten to mention it," Catherine said. "Anyway, that was pretty impressive. Matthew's only told me about the extraction process, but I've never seen it. Didn't you think it was cool, Chrissy?"

"Uh, yeah." Was she the only one feeling awkward? She

avoided Jason's eyes, but she could feel him looking at her, as if in challenge. Or maybe it was anger.

"Well, maybe Ben can show you the rest of the mines. The smelting area's just in the next cavern, you should go see it. If you'll excuse me, I have to check on a couple of things." He turned and walked away from them.

Christina let out a breath. Maybe it was better this way. Better for them to ignore each other. But the knot in her stomach remained.

Her words last night had been harsh and judgmental. They had just come spewing out of her mouth as she battled her emotions. Lust. Anger. Jealousy. Seeing him with that other woman had brought up something in her she had never felt before and she wanted to get back at him. Of course, she didn't expect him to kiss her and touch her like that.

"Chrissy?" Catherine shot her a concerned look. "Ready to go?"

"Yeah, sure."

They followed Ben down a set of small caverns and walkways until they came to another large cavern. This one was just as big as the last one, but instead of the quiet atmosphere, it was ear-splittingly loud. The sound of metal against metal was unmistakable. Large, heavy industrial equipment was set up all around and the temperature in here was much hotter. Perspiration broke out on her brow and upper lip as she felt the sweltering heat all around her.

"This is the smelting floor," Ben explained, raising his voice so they could hear him. "We take the blackstone in here and melt it down to a more usable form."

"Don't you have a separate facility?" Catherine asked. "Like a plant in town?"

Ben shook his head. "If the blackstone cools after dragon

fire extracts it, it becomes weaker. If we want the hardest and purest form, the smelting has to happen while it's still hot. So we gotta move quick. That's why we set up this system each time we move sites. This is the previous site where we've already extracted the vein. Good thing is that there's so much blackstone in the mountains that we only have to move every one or two years."

They followed him, staying at the edge of the cavern, watching as the workers pulled massive carts filled with black rocks before dumping them onto a moving conveyor belt. The rocks traveled through a series of machines, before moving into several giant metal pots. The inside of the pots glowed a bright yellow orange.

"Once we've extracted the blackstone—" Ben stopped short when a loud, screeching sound rang out through the cave, drowning out the rest of the din. He turned and his eyes widened. "What the—"

One of the chains that had been holding up a huge smelting pot had broken and dangled overhead. As they watched, the pot began to tip over, threatening to pour out the burning liquid inside.

"GET OUT!" Ben's inhuman roar reverberated throughout the cavern. "Move!"

There were shouts and yells, and the sickening sound of metal screeching against metal made Christina's teeth hurt. The air grew hotter around her, but she couldn't move. She froze, watching the smelting pot as it began to overturn.

She closed her eyes and braced herself. But, instead of burning hot metal, she only felt the whip of air. When she opened her eyes, she saw a massive gold figure in front of her, its wings beating madly. *Jason!*

The dragon's claws held the smelting pot, roaring as it kept the hot liquid from spilling over. It wrenched the pot down from the remaining chains then set it on the floor, holding it in place.

"We need support!" Ben shouted to the crew. "Get whatever you can to hold that thing in place!"

Christina gasped as suddenly, a massive grizzly bear ripped out of Ben's human body. Massive was an understatement. She'd never seen bears in real life, but she was pretty sure they didn't grow to fifteen feet tall. The bear let out an angry roar.

Two more bears, smaller than Ben but still intimidating, ran toward them dragging massive chains. The two of them wrapped them around the pot, and the grizzly grabbed the ends, pulling on it then secured it to the nearest post. Several people came forward, dragging more equipment, probably to weld the chains into place. The dragon staggered back.

"Jason!" Christina screamed, watching as the dragon began to shrink back to human form. He fell back, his body hitting the ground with a thud. *No!*

She ran to him, kneeling down next to his body. His eyes were closed and he was covered in sweat. And his hands—Oh God, his hands—they were red and raw, and the sight made bile rise up her throat.

"Medic!" Ben shouted. She didn't even realize he had transformed back. He knelt down next to her and patted her shoulder. "I know it looks bad, but he'll survive. It's just a scratch."

Shock ran through her system. She knew Ben was right; she'd seen worse on other shifters and they'd survived. But looking at Jason injured made her heart wrench.

Ben let out a throaty growl. "Goddamit." He ran a hand through this thick, dark hair.

"What's the matter?" Christina asked.

He sighed. "This doesn't happen often. In fact, this is only the second major accident we've had in a long time."

"And the first?"

"It was two days ago."

A cold chill ran down Christina's spine. She had arrived two days ago. A thought crossed her mind, but before she could fully flesh out the scenario, shouts and screams from the other side of the cave distracted her.

"Boss! Boss!" Two burly men came toward them, dragging a smaller figure between them. "We found this guy trying to run out of the cave. He's not one of ours."

"Yeah," the other one said. "Human."

They tossed the man to the ground, and Ben reached down, wrapped his massive hands around the guy's shirt and lifted him up. "Who the hell are you?"

The man should have been afraid. Even in human form, Ben could probably snap his neck in half and who knows what he could do as a grizzly. But the man's face widened into a sick smile. "You're dirty, filthy animals," he spat. "*Abominations*. You need to be erased from this earth."

"You motherfucker!" Ben shook him hard. "Who are you with?"

"You won't live long enough to find out," the man said with a grin. "We will take every single one of you out."

Ben tossed him back to the ground. "Lock up this son of a bitch and call Blackstone P.D.," he roared at the two workers. They nodded and dragged the man away as he continued to spew out vile insults.

Despite the heat in the cave, icy fingers seeped into Christina's veins. The man's words … she had heard it all before. It was what those anti-shifter groups would shout and spew at rallies and protests. She'd heard worse, actually.

Could someone from one of those groups have followed her here? The Agency had always worked clandestinely, keeping their existence secret. But maybe after all these years, those anti-shifter groups had gotten wise.

"Chrissy?" Catherine asked as she knelt down beside her. "Are you okay?"

"Yeah, I'm fine." The answer was almost automatic. She looked down at Jason. His eyes were still shut, but his breathing was even. A closer look at his hands told her he was already healing and she sighed with relief. What if his injuries had been worse? Or if he had been too late?

"We should give him some room," Catherine said, gently tugging at her hand.

"Huh?" She looked up and saw two men carrying medical bags coming their way. "Right." She followed her sister outside.

There was nothing she could do now and Jason would be fine. The thought made that tightness in her chest loosen somewhat. But, it wasn't over. She had to call her father and brothers right away.

CHAPTER 9

"How you feelin' cuz?"

Jason opened his eyes and let out a groan. The pain in his hands made him jolt. He raised them to his face and winced. "Like ass," he said with a sigh.

"It looks much better," Ben said, peering down at his palms.

"You mean, better than raw beef?"

His cousin chuckled. "Well, you're back to making jokes, so you must be doing all right. The doctor said you should be fully healed by tonight." Ben's face darkened. "If you didn't swoop in on time, who knows what would have happened."

Jason shot up. "Christina—and Catherine," he quickly added.

"They're back at the castle. I had Luke take them home."

He let go of the breath he was holding, his body relaxing. He had been in shock, seeing Christina so soon after last night. Her rejection had stung worse than any pain, even the one he was feeling now. Having her standing in front of him was too much, and he'd had to walk away.

But when he heard the commotion coming from the smelting room, instinct took over. Sensing that Christina was in danger, he raced toward her. He got there in time, just as that pot was about to pour hot liquid metal all over the floor. His dragon ripped out of him and though the pain had been nearly unbearable, it had been worth it knowing Christina and everyone else was safe.

"What happened?"

Ben's face got even darker. "You were right. Someone's out to get us. We caught some guy sneaking away. Haven't gotten a confession yet, but we have him locked up. P.D.'s on the way to pick him up."

His inner dragon roared, urging him to go find the man and rip his head off for nearly killing Christina. *Not until we find out who's trying to sabotage us*, he told the animal. But, he promised his dragon, they would get their revenge.

"Hey, hey!" Ben stepped forward as Jason tried to get up. "You gotta get some rest."

"I'm fine," he said as he reached for the spare set of clothes at the foot of the bed. Gingerly, he got dressed. "I want to see this guy before Chief Meacham takes him away."

Ben shrugged and led him out of the medical RV then to one of the trailers across the lot which housed their supplies. Two of their guys were standing in front, guarding the door. When Ben and Jason approached, they stepped aside to let them in.

"We should still be careful," Ben warned as he turned the knob and walked inside. "He's unstable and ... motherfucker!"

The metallic smell was unmistakable. A body was slumped on the ground in a pool of blood. Next to it was a pair of scissors, also covered in blood.

"Fucker!" Ben cursed and slammed his fist on the wall.

Jason had never seen him so agitated, though he understood. That man had tried to hurt their crew. Even if Christina and Catherine hadn't been there, if any of their workers had died, there would have been hell to pay.

"He was working alone?" Jason asked.

"As far as we could tell. But no way he could have done all that by himself."

"He had help," Jason concluded. "I'll tell Matthew. We're gonna have to double up on security around here." The sound of sirens outside signaled the arrival of the Blackstone P.D. "Go talk to Chief Meacham," he told Ben as they walked out to the trailer. He turned to the two men outside. "Don't let anyone except P.D. come in here, okay?"

Jason walked away from the trailer, his mind reeling. This was big. Someone was really out to hurt them. But who? And why did this man kill himself? He guessed it was so they wouldn't be able to get more answers from him.

He made his way back to the middle trailer, where he and Matthew had their on-site offices. It was a good thing he always left his cell phone inside before going into the mines. As he reached for his phone which was sitting on the desk, it began to ring. *Probably Matthew.*

Not bothering to look at the caller ID, he picked up right away. "Jason Lennox."

"Jason," the breathy voice on the other end said. "I've been trying to get a hold of you all day."

"Jessica?" Why the hell was she calling? Sure, he walked out on their date, but she didn't bother waiting for him to come back. He had been gone a few minutes.

"I should be mad at you, but how can I be angry when you're taking me to the hottest social event of the year."

What the fuck is she talking about? "I am?"

"Yes, silly! As if you didn't know. Everyone wants an invite to your brother's wedding."

"When did I invite you?"

Jessica laughed. "Last night. Oh, stop joking around. Remember, I asked if you had a date to the wedding and you shook your head. Then, I asked if you would take me and you said yes."

Jason felt a headache begin to build in his temple. He tried to recall what happened last night and he vaguely remembered saying yes to some question. *Shit.* "Uhm... Jessica...see—"

"You're not backing out, are you? Did you find another date?"

"What? No." Technically that was true.

"Good. I was going to ask you what I should wear."

He really didn't have time for this. "Whatever. I mean, whatever you choose should be fine."

"Great! I was thinking of this strappy dress that I saw..."

He let her drone on for a few minutes, tuning her out halfway. *Well, would it be that bad?* Jessica was a beautiful woman, he couldn't deny that. And he'd asked her out initially to distract himself from Christina who obviously wanted nothing to do with him. Why should he live like a fucking monk? This was what he wanted, right? No mate, just keep living his damn life the way he had been doing the last years.

"Sorry, babe," he said, cutting her off in the middle of her monologue about nail polish. "I have to go."

"Right. Well, I'll see you at the wedding."

He breathed a sigh of relief when she hung up, but inside, he was fighting his inner dragon. It was furious, and didn't want anything to do with Jessica. He was tempted to phone her back and call the whole thing off just to have some peace. But, there were much more important things to think about right now. He dialed Matthew's number.

CHAPTER 10

As soon as she got back to Blackstone Castle, Christina contacted her eldest brother, Xander, and relayed the story to him. Her family was already on their way to Colorado for the wedding and would be there the next day, so they agreed to talk about it face-to-face when they arrived.

And now, it was the day before the wedding. Papa, Xander, Kostas, Nikos, and Cordy had arrived together sometime after lunch. Needless to say, they all had an emotional reunion with Catherine, whom her siblings had not seen in a year. There was lots of crying (mostly Cordelia and Catherine), hugs, teasing, and apologies. Christina herself could not help but be emotional and finally, after the first time in months, that ache that had been building in her heart was starting to fill again.

"Christina? Do I look okay?" a shy voice asked.

Christina looked up as her youngest sister exited the bathroom. It had been too long since they'd spent time together. Cordy had insisted on staying with her in the guest room.

"Of course you do, *kardia mou*." It was their nickname for their youngest sibling. *My heart.* It not only matched her name, but who she was. Cordelia truly was the one thing that kept them all together, first through Mama's death and then Catherine's departure.

Sixteen-year-old Cordelia Stavros frowned. "I'm too chubby for this outfit." She looked down at the pink dress. It was a bit stretched out around her middle, and a tad too long. Christina thought it also looked a bit too old fashioned, but she didn't mind. She was horrified whenever she saw what teenagers wore these days and was glad Cordy didn't dress that way.

"I wish you'd stop saying that." Christina rose to her feet and walked over to her sister, placing a hand on her shoulder. "You are not chubby. You're beautiful. You just haven't lost your baby fat, that's all." Despite being a wolf shifter, Cordy's body tended to be on the … generous side. "You'll grow out of it."

Cordelia's face fell. "You have to say that. You're my sister."

Christina let out a sigh. Cordy had already been a shy child and growing up isolated on an island didn't help her confidence. Though she seemed happy about studying in England, Christina suspected her life outside her classes was less than ideal. "You look great."

"I should have lost some weight before I came here," Cordy stared unhappily at herself in the full-length mirror. "Headmistress Anna said I should stop having dessert after dinner."

Christina wanted nothing more than to put Headmistress Anna in a sleeper hold, but she settled on writing a strongly-worded email tonight. "You're perfect the way you are." She kissed the top of her head. "Now, why don't I do your hair and put on a little bit of makeup, then we can go down together?"

Her face lit up. "Thanks. You always know how to style my hair." She hugged Christina. "I missed you so much."

"Me too."

She swept Cordelia's fine blonde hair into a sophisticated updo, put a little bit of blush on her cheeks and gloss on her lips. Cordelia was blessed with gorgeous skin, the perfect mix between the English rose complexion of their mother and ruddy Mediterranean tan of their father, so she didn't need much makeup. When she finished, Cordy beamed at her, her eyes shining with joy.

"Ready?" Christina asked.

"I guess."

"If you're tired or bored, just tell me okay? We don't have to stay long."

They walked out to the main part of the castle, down the stairs, and to the formal dining room. Since the Stavroses were arriving so close to the wedding, Matthew and Catherine decided on an early dinner engagement party served in the dining room and then drinks, coffee, and dessert in the library afterward. Everyone was already sitting down to dinner by the time Christina and Cordy walked in.

Matthew's parents, Riva and Hank, had flown in the night before. She, Matthew, Catherine, and Sybil had a quiet dinner with them in the East wing. It was quite a difference from tonight's dinner. There were so many more people, some Christina had never met. At the head of the table, Hank and Riva Lennox sat with her father and Xander. They were all chatting and laughing.

They were a bit late and since the seating arrangement was casual, the only spots left were near the other end. Not that she minded. Jason was next to Matthew near the head, and he didn't even notice her and Cordy slip in. She sat next to Luke Lennox, with Cordy on her right.

"Hello, Luke, nice to see you again," she greeted. She had

formally met the last Lennox sibling the day before. He'd just arrived at the mines when the accident happened, and Ben arranged to have him drive her and Catherine back to the castle. He was a shifter; a lion, Catherine explained later when they were alone. He was actually Riva and Hank's adopted son.

"Oh, this is my sister, Cordy," Christina introduced.

"Hey," Luke said with a brief glance at Cordelia. He took a sip of his wine then went back to staring ahead with his tawny eyes.

During the drive back from the mines, Luke had barely looked at her and hardly said a word the entire time, so she didn't really expect any riveting conversation from him. *At least he acknowledged Cordelia*, she thought. Not that her sister noticed. She was too preoccupied with her shoes.

The dinner was delicious as always. Meg had prepared a full, six-course meal that had everyone singing her praises. Another couple joined them at their end of the table, friends of Hank and Riva from Blackstone town. Christina urged Cordelia to talk a bit, but she seemed nervous. It was ironic that her sister who spoke six languages could hardly find two words to say in front of company. She just hoped she would grow out of it.

Finally, when everyone had finished the scrumptious meal, Hank stood up and offered a heartwarming toast to Matthew and Catherine before inviting everyone to the library.

As Christina stood up, she saw Xander signal to her. She nodded and turned to her sister. "Cordy, why don't you go ahead, I have to get something from the room."

"But—"

"Papa and Catherine will be there. I miss you a lot, but you haven't spent much time with Catherine. We're leaving right after the wedding and you won't see her again for a few months." From the corner of her eye, she saw Nikos slip into one of the rooms in the hallway.

"All right," Cordy said, mollified for the moment. "Don't be too long, okay?"

"I won't."

She watched Cordy walk up ahead, and then slowed her steps. She pivoted and turned back. When she got to the other room, all of her brothers were there.

"I've briefed Kostas and Nikos on our conversation," Xander said. "Did you find out anything else?"

"Only that the man they caught is definitely dead. Killed himself while he was being detained."

Kostas frowned. "Like the guy from SPHK."

She nodded. A few months ago, while they were on a case to stop a bombing at a shifter community center in London, they were able to catch the man who had planted the explosives. It turned out he was part of the Society for the Protection of Human Kind, one of the oldest anti-shifter groups in existence. But before they could interrogate the guy, he had killed himself with a poison pill he carried in his pocket.

It had been a strange case, because SPHK was more of a political lobbying group, not one known for violence. The attempted bombing had been all over the news, but the president of SPHK denied that they had anything to do with it. The Agency couldn't prove otherwise, as the only concrete connection they had between the attempted bombing and the SPHK was dead.

"But why would they come here?" Nikos asked.

"Easy," Kostas said. "Blackstone is a haven for people like us, especially since it's protected by dragons. No one can touch the Lennoxes."

"Exactly," Xander said. "Aside from a few smear campaigns, anti-shifter groups have stayed away from dragons. Most know not to mess with them."

"Still, the day of the first accident coinciding with my arrival? There has to be a connection," Christina pointed out.

"Were you followed?" Xander asked.

She thought for a moment. "No … I don't think so. Plus, my cover is solid." Few people knew she and her sisters existed. Papa made sure of that by keeping them away from the public eye for many years. When she and Catherine went to boarding school in England, they registered under their old last name, Archer.

"We'll have to consider every possibility then," Kostas said. "The dead man. Do you know what he looks like? Where is the body?"

"I know the police department came after the accident," Christina said. "They should have taken him to the morgue, but I can find out for sure."

"All right." Xander checked his watch. "We've been gone too long. Let's head to the library, but not all at the same time." They nodded in agreement.

Christina arrived at the library last. She had gone back up to her room, changed her shoes and put on some lipstick, just in case anyone was suspicious of why she was gone so long. She scanned the room, looking for her sister. She hoped Cordy wasn't too upset or anxious without her.

A familiar laugh made her whip around. Her sister was standing by the fireplace talking to … Jason? She did a double take. Yes, that was definitely Jason standing next to her sister.

She frowned. *What the bloody hell was going on?* She marched over to them. "Cordy?" she asked. "Are you okay? Do you want to go back upstairs?" Her eyes narrowed at Jason. "What are you doing?"

"Christina," Cordy warned.

"Hey now." He raised his hands. She tried to ignore the fact that he looked handsome in his casual suit jacket and his dark hair slicked back. "I saw a pretty lady standing all by her lonesome and thought I'd keep her company." He smiled at Cordy. "You don't mind, do you, Cordy?"

Cordy shook her head. "Of course not."

Mild shock went through her system. Her sister was actually talking to someone and ... smiling? Yes, that was definitely a genuine smile on her face.

"Cordy was teaching me how to swear in four languages." He winked at Cordy.

"Six, actually," Cordy corrected proudly. "And a couple of other ones I learned from some of my roommates."

"She told me what *vlaca* means," Jason said, tsking at Christina.

"That's not very nice of you to call him that," her sister scolded.

Christina gave him a smirk. "I assure you he deserved it at the time."

Cordy turned back to him, her brows furrowed together.

"I agree and I've apologized," Jason said gallantly.

"Cordy!" Catherine called from across the room. She walked over to them and tugged at her younger sister's arm. "You haven't met Matthew's mom and dad yet. They've been dying to be introduced to you."

"All right. I'll talk to you later, Jason," she said with a shy smile.

"I look forward to it." He gave her an exaggerated bow.

As she watched her sister blush, Christina couldn't believe

what she had witnessed. Jason had managed to put her sister at ease and make her smile. She supposed that was natural to him, with all the women he went after, but there was nothing but brotherly affection in the way he'd interacted with Cordy.

"What?" Jason said.

She blinked. "Huh?"

"What's that look?"

"Look?"

He puffed out an exasperated breath. "That look you're giving me. Did I grow a second head or something?"

Something like that. "Nothing. I mean, thank you. For keeping Cordy company."

"She's a lovely girl," Jason said. "Very sweet, though a little shy. I saw her standing by herself and thought that she's probably bored to tears around all these adults."

"She grew up alone," Christina explained. "She's not used to being around so many new strangers."

"She had you didn't she?"

His question puzzled her. "What do you mean?"

"She's only a couple of years younger than you, right? So you were around her a lot."

"I guess. We had different tutors of course. But yeah, we played with her, helped take care of her. I even read her stories in bed until she was thirteen and decided she was getting too old to be tucked in."

"So you're kind of like her mother?"

She smiled. "More like a nagging aunt."

Jason laughed. "But you were there for her," he said, his voice turning serious.

"I … Mama died right after she was born." A lump was forming in her throat.

"It's okay," Jason said in a soft voice. "Catherine told me."

She looked up at him, unnerved by his silvery stare, but at the same time, couldn't tear her eyes away. For a moment, it seemed like there was no one else in the room. The memories from the other night came flooding back, and lust spiraled through her. She remembered the feel of his lips on hers, the stubble on his jaw tickling her sensitive skin. His hands and, God, those fingers as he stroked her to orgasm.

His nostrils flared and his eyes darkened. Was he thinking the same thing?

Christina forced herself to look away. She cleared her throat.

"I—"

"Chris—" he said at the same time.

"Yes—"

"We—"

They both paused then he spoke. "Sorry," he ran his fingers through his thick, dark hair. "I mean, you go first."

She took a deep breath. "I just wanted to say I'm glad you're not hurt. And thank you for saving me and Catherine."

"Ah, well, I couldn't let anything happen to you ... or anyone."

"Of course," she nodded. She pushed away the thought that she wished he had done it for her. Because that would be silly of course. He was the boss, the protector of Blackstone. It was his job to keep everyone there safe.

The awkward silence stretched between them and she didn't know if she preferred that or the sexual tension that had been brewing earlier. Finally, she saw her way out when she spied Cordy from the corner of her eye. Her sister hid a big yawn behind her hand and her eyelids had begun to droop. "Looks like someone has a bad case of jet lag," she remarked. "She needs her rest before tomorrow. I should go."

"Right," Jason said, then shoved his hands into the pockets of his pants.

She turned, but before she could walk away, a warm hand wrapped around her arm. An involuntary shiver went through her. "Yes?" she asked.

Silvery eyes raked over her. "Christina, I ... Goodnight."

She nodded. "Goodnight, Jason."

CHAPTER 11

"THIS IS IT, BRO," Jason said as he helped Matthew with the tie on his tuxedo. "Are you really going to go through with it? I'm pretty sure you can still back out before you say 'I do'."

Matthew laughed. "Yeah, I'm sure. She's the one, man."

Jason gave him a tight smile. "I'm happy for you. I really am."

"You know, you can be happy too," Matthew said in a quiet voice. "I know I said I wouldn't push it, but Chris—"

"Oh my, don't you look handsome!" Riva exclaimed as she walked in with Hank. She looked beautiful in her pale lavender dress, while Hank looked distinguished in his tux. "I can't believe my baby is getting married."

Jason sighed inwardly with relief. *Saved by Mom.* He really didn't want to listen to Matthew give him a hard time about Christina. He already had enough of that from his own dragon.

"*Mom—*" Matthew began as she came up to brush some lint off his tux.

"I know what you're going to say, but you'll always be my baby." She looked at Jason with tears in her eyes. "All of you."

"You'll have to forgive your mother," Hank said dryly. "She hasn't stopped crying since she unearthed your baby shoes from storage yesterday."

"Oh, Hank," she said, swatting him on the arm. But her eyes shone with love for her mate. "Go call Sybil and Luke. I need family pictures."

Matthew rolled his eyes, but Riva paid him no mind. As soon as they were all in the bedroom, Riva made them all pose together for pictures, snapping away with her camera phone. Much to Jason's surprise, even Luke participated, though he was scowling in most of the pictures. He wondered if his adopted brother had changed his mind after all these years of staying away. Maybe even Luke wasn't immune to weddings. He'd even worn the matching tux Matthew had gotten for them all.

"Almost ready?" Meg's face popped in through the doorway. "Everyone's here and seated." She turned to Jason. "Even your date is here. She must have asked me ten times where you were."

"Your date?" Matthew raised a brow at him.

"You have a girlfriend?" Riva asked, excitement in her eyes. "Why didn't you tell me?"

"She's not my girlfriend," he said sourly. "Just a date. This is a wedding, right? People bring dates to these things all the time."

"But this is a family affair," Sybil pointed out. "Are you introducing her to us?"

Hank cleared his throat. "C'mon now, let's leave Jason alone. And we need to get going."

Jason shot his father a grateful look and followed the rest

of his family as they filed out of Matthew's bedroom and out of the castle.

With spring just around the corner and the weather finally getting milder, Matthew and Catherine decided to have an outdoor ceremony on the back lawn, though the reception would be in the Grand Ballroom since it was still cold in the evenings.

The ceremony area was cordoned off with swathes of white cloth, interspersed with pastel colors. There were rows of chairs and an aisle down the middle decorated with flowers and cloth in the same spring color theme. At the front was a raised dais with an arch made of flowers. Judge Cornelius Atherton was waiting there, dressed in his black robes.

Matthew took his place in front with Jason beside him as his best man. Hank and Riva took their seats on the groom's side.

The orchestra began to play and everyone sat down. The bridesmaids and groomsmen came out first, Sybil and Luke, Nate and Kate, and Amelia and Ben. When Jason saw a flash of blonde hair turn the corner, he held his breath.

Christina walked down the aisle by herself. She was wearing a light-blue dress with delicate straps. The fabric around the torso clung to the curves of her firm breasts, and exposed just a hint of cleavage. Her long, golden hair shone as it tumbled past her creamy shoulders. He'd never seen anyone look as stunning as she did in that moment. They locked eyes and she quickly turned away, a blush staining her cheeks.

Last night had given him hope as he swore he could not only see the wanting in her eyes when she looked at him, but smell her arousal. As she came closer, she glanced at him one more time then took her position opposite him on the dais.

Behind her, Cordy, as second maid of honor, finished her walk. Jason gave her a wink and she beamed a smile at him.

The music changed and a hush went over the crowd. Soon, the bride and her father were walking down the aisle. Catherine looked radiant in her white gown and he heard Matthew's breath hitch. She was a beautiful bride, but Jason couldn't help but be drawn to Christina, who was staring at her sister as tears glistened down her heart-shaped face. Soon, the ceremony was on its way, with the bride and groom up front and their attendants beside them.

"Jason," Luke whispered from his left, his voice barely perceptible.

"What?" he asked, glancing at his brother.

"Do you hear that?" Luke asked, his thick blond brows drawing into a frown.

"Huh? Hear what?"

Matthew glared at them then turned back to Judge Atherton. That quickly shut them up. But a few seconds later, Luke called his attention again.

"Jason—"

"Shut up," he hissed. From the bride's side, Sybil shot them a warning look.

"I swear, I hear something. Like a buzzing sound," Luke said. "Don't you hear it?"

"No, dude," Jason said. "Now pipe down." God, what the hell was wrong with Luke?

"And so," Judge Atherton continued, "should anyone here present know of any reason that this couple should not be joined in marriage, speak now or forever hold your peace."

Luke's voice cut through the reverent silence. "Everyone get away! Now!"

"What the hell?" Matthew exclaimed. A murmur rushed

through the crowd. In the front row, Hank was getting to his feet, while Catherine's family looked at each other with puzzled expressions.

Jason whipped around, ready to face Luke and take him down if it came to that. He expected to see a crazed expression on his brother's face, but all he saw was clear determination. Something was up. "What's wrong?"

Luke growled at the Judge, Matthew, and Catherine. "Leave. Get off this stage! You're all in danger."

The determination in his voice struck Jason like hammer. "Do as he says. Now!"

Matthew rushed everyone off, with Ben and Nathan helping. Meanwhile, Luke was already bending down, his hands digging under the wooden boards, before he lifted the entire dais off. He flipped it over with one motion.

"Fuck!" Jason cursed when he saw what was underneath. There was a suitcase-sized package wrapped in duct tape. Attached to it was a large, red digital display that ticked down every passing second. Three minutes and five seconds.

He heard Matthew swear loudly before turning to the guests. "Everyone, please go back into the castle. It's not safe here."

A buzz rang through the crowd, and a few people rushed to get up. Matthew put an arm around Catherine and whispered to her. Together, they gathered the groomsmen and bridesmaids then dispersed, helping people off the lawn and into the castle.

"What's going on?" Christina rushed over and then her gaze landed on the bomb. "Oh, my God."

Jason grabbed her by the arms. "Get out of here, Christina. Go back inside with everyone."

"No!" she protested. "We need to diffuse it. What are you doing?"

Jason was taking off his jacket. "I'm going to fly it away," he said. He checked the dial. Two minutes and thirty seconds. He could clear the mountain in that time.

"You can't!" she said, wrapping her fists around the collar of his jacket.

"I have to," he said. "It'll be okay. There's a lake a few miles from here. I can drop it there."

"And if you don't make it?" Blue eyes searched his. "No. Nikos!" she called to her brother.

The youngest Stavros brother ran toward them, and as soon as he saw the bomb, he nodded to Christina. "I'm on it."

"On it?" Jason asked, confused. "What do you mean, on it?"

Nikos knelt down next to the bomb, and took out a small pouch from his pocket. Xander and Kostas followed, speaking rapidly in Greek as they approached Nikos.

"What the hell is going on?" Jason asked Christina.

She hesitated. "Nikos trained with the Greek Special Forces. He's done this before."

Jason's gut told him that wasn't the entire truth, but that wasn't important. "You have to go, Christina. Go somewhere safe."

"I won't leave you," she said, desperation in her voice as she clung to him. "Don't make me go, please."

Her words struck something in him, and while he didn't want to be away from her, he knew he had to get her to safety. He looked back at the Stavros brothers who were now examining the bomb. "What are they saying?"

"They're working on it. Nikos keeps saying something about the timer and fuse ... a couple of kilos of C-4 ... enough to level the castle." Her face grew pale.

"Dammit!" He looked around and saw Nate a few feet away. "Nate! Get everyone back to town! Now!" Nate nodded and ran toward the castle.

"How much longer?" he asked.

"Less than one minute," Kostas called.

"He won't be able to diffuse it in time," Jason said. And he wouldn't have much time to get away now. But if he flew as high as he could ... "Christina, please let go. I need to do this."

"You can't. You won't make it."

"But everyone else will," he said in a quiet voice. *You will.*

"Jason..." she reached down to take his hands, lacing her fingers through his. She closed her eyes. "I—"

"It's done!" Nikos said and whooped. "Yes!" He jumped up and raised his fist in the air. "*Opa!*" His brothers slapped him on the back.

Christina's eyes flew open, her pink lips parted. She looked up at him and her shoulders sank with relief. "I..." She turned red, dropped his hands, and trudged toward her brothers. Jason stood there for a moment, his heart slowing down as he realized how close they had been in that moment. He took a deep breath and followed her.

"How did you know?" Jason turned to Luke as he stood next to the three brothers who were now examining the bomb.

"That high-pitched sound. You really couldn't hear it?" Luke asked. "It was driving me nuts."

Jason shook his head. "No, couldn't hear a thing."

"You're a lion shifter, right?" Kostas asked. Luke nodded. "Cat hearing. You can hear higher frequencies than most animals. Even wolves."

"I'll be damned," Luke said, shaking his head.

"Are you sure it's diffused?" Jason asked. Nikos nodded in the affirmative. "We should call Blackstone P.D., just in case."

"And we need to find out who did this," Matthew said as he approached them from behind.

"Where's Catherine? And Cordy?" Christina asked. "Papa? Are they okay?"

"They're safe," he said. "I saw them off in the limo with Mom, Dad, and the rest of the girls."

Christina released a breath, her shoulders sagging in relief. "Thank God."

"Don't call anyone back yet," Xander said. "There may still be other bombs around."

The thought made Jason clench his fists in anger. "We need to sweep the place. The rangers might be able to help," he said, referring to the Blackstone Rangers who were in charge of protecting the mountains. "They have a few big cat shifters on their team too."

"Can't hear anything else around here, but I'll start looking around," Luke said, as he began to take off his jacket. "I'll be faster on four feet." He stalked off into the distance, discarding his clothes as he disappeared into the tree line.

The sounds of approaching sirens broke the silence in the air. "That'll be Meacham," Matthew said. "We should go talk to him. Get everything sorted out."

Jason glanced over at Christina and her brothers, who were quietly talking amongst themselves. The feeling that something was not quite right kept nagging at him. Christina turned her head and locked eyes with him, but quickly looked away. *Something was definitely going on.*

"Jason," Matthew called. "Are you coming?"

"Yeah. Right behind you."

CHAPTER 12

"WHAT CAN you tell us about the bomb?" Xander asked in a low voice as soon as Jason and Matthew disappeared into the house.

"Nothing much right now," Nikos said with a shake of his head. "Standard timer and C-4 explosives. Probably timed to go off sometime during the ceremony. We were extremely lucky they used a clock that emitted a frequency the lion shifter could hear."

"Where did it come from? And who made it?"

"I'll have to take it apart in the lab back at Headquarters to find a signature, if there is one," Nikos explained. "Think anyone will notice if we sneak it off?"

"Their police department will surely want to take it into their custody," Kostas said. "And anything else they find."

Xander turned to Christina. "What's your plan for getting more information from the cops?"

"Still working on it," she answered. She chewed her lip, deep in thought. Frankly, she really couldn't get her head together at the moment. The thought of losing Jason tore at her insides. Her hands still shook, even though it hadn't come to that.

"Let's keep an eye on things," Xander said. "Try to lay low, but gather as much intelligence as we can. This must be SPHK, DARSA, or one of the other groups."

"But how did they get this in here?" Nikos asked, gesturing to the diffused bomb. The numbers on the display read '00:23', and thinking of how close they came to death shot ice through Christina's veins.

"Caterers, flower arrangers, decorators, the band..." Xander shook his head. "There were dozens of people going in and out here during the last twenty-four hours. It could have been any of them, or someone who was paid to take it in."

"Why go through all this trouble?" Kostas asked. "What was their plan?"

"To kill as many shifters as they could in one place, of course," Xander said, his voice edgy.

"But, did they target us or the Lennoxes?" Kostas posed.

"There's no way anyone within five feet of that bomb would have survived," Nikos said. "Not even shifters."

"That makes sense," Kostas said. "It was probably the first major event where all four of them were present and guaranteed to be next to each other. Same with us, if we were the target."

Hot anger poured through Christina's veins. "Those bastards," she said through gritted teeth.

"We'll get them," Xander said. "And then they will pay. For everything."

She nodded, swallowing the lump in her throat. "I should go check on what's going on. Catherine will be distraught."

"Take care of her," Xander said. "She will need you."

Christina picked up her skirts and marched toward the direction of the castle. When she got inside, there were dozens of police officers roaming about. Matthew, Jason, and Hank were in the corner, talking to an older man in uniform who must have been the chief.

An idea popped into her head. "Excuse me," she said, stopping a young officer as she passed by. "Would you by any chance ... I mean, is Deputy Carson around?"

The officer nodded. "Over there, ma'am." She pointed to the tall, uniformed man who was directing a few of the cops.

"Thank you," she said before sauntering over to Carson. "Deputy," she called in a breathy voice. She nearly gagged thinking about how it made her sound like a bimbo, but men seemed to like it. "Deputy Carson, do you remember me?"

The handsome deputy turned around, his face lighting up with recognition as he saw her. "Yes, ma'am," he said, "Ms. Stavros."

"Yes," she said. "Please, call me Christina."

"All right, then you should call me Cole," he said with a grin. "What can I do for you?"

"Oh you must be busy, but..." She shuddered. "This whole thing, terrible, right?" She reached out and placed a hand on his bicep and squeezed. "I'm just glad you— all of you—are here now."

"We're just doing our job, ma'am, er, I mean, Christina."

"Yes, and great job, too." She looked up at him through lowered lashes. "You haven't found any other bombs or anything else?"

"Not yet, but our guys are working on it. If we find anything, we'll have our bomb squad ready."

She clapped her hands together. "Oh good. Is there a chance that bomb can go off? What will happen to it?"

"Your brother did a good job diffusing it. It was such good luck that he'd been trained as a bomb expert. But, no, it won't go off. We'll be taking it to our forensic lab down at the police station to examine it and anything else we find."

"Oh thank God," she exclaimed.

"Christina!"

She turned around. Sybil was running toward her, her face pale. The young woman barreled into her and engulfed her in a hug. "Thank God you're okay."

Kate wasn't too far behind. "Chrissy! You survived!" She slapped her on the shoulder. "I'd hate to have lost you. We still have so many nights of tequila shots ahead of us."

She disentangled herself from Sybil. "I'm fine. Everything's going to be fine." She could have lost them too, her new friends. Anger raged inside her. "Where's Catherine? Cordy? Are they all right?"

"In your room. They're good. Catherine's sad. Angry. Depressed."

"She's going through the stages of grief mighty quick," Kate quipped.

"Sybil. Kate." Cole greeted them. "You girls okay?"

"Yeah, we're good," Kate said, then shot Christina a look. "What are you—"

"Excuse me, Deputy." Another officer came up from behind them. "Chief Meacham wants to talk to you."

"Right." He turned to Christina. "If you'll excuse me…"

"Of course." She said and then patted him on the arm. "Thank you again." He gave her a nod before walking off with the other officer.

Wheels began to turn in her mind. They had to get the bomb back to The Agency headquarters. Or at least, get a copy of the forensic report. If The Agency were an official entity it would have been easy to work with the P.D., but since they weren't, they had to resort to less than legal tactics. If she could only get more information somehow.

Kate let out a whistle. "Woohoo. You go, girl." She fanned herself. "Look at that man's ass in those tight khakis. I swear, I love a man in uniform."

"You hate cops," Sybil pointed out. "But," she turned to Christina, "what were you talking about?"

"Uhm, nothing. We were just getting reacquainted. We met the last time I was here."

"That man is *ffffiiiiiiiiiine*," Kate exclaimed. She raised her hand for a high-five and Sybil rolled her eyes.

"Well, I should go check on Catherine."

Christina made her way toward the grand staircase that led to the upper level. As she walked up the steps, she felt eyes on her and she whipped around. From across the room, Jason stared at her, an inscrutable look on his face, his jaw tense. Did he suspect anything about her brothers? About her? It had been a close call, and they had no choice but to have Nikos diffuse the bomb. But then again, that might have raised too many suspicions. She only hoped that they could come up with a better explanation next time.

Despite what happened, they managed to salvage what was left of the day. Once Blackstone P.D. and the Rangers declared that the whole town and mountains were clear, almost everyone came back to the castle. Judge Atherton married Matthew and Catherine in the library in front of the family and close friends, and the reception continued in the Grand Ballroom as planned.

Spirits were surprisingly high at the party as the band played and the champagne flowed, the events of that morning seemingly forgotten. Christina had not seen Jason since the ceremony. She didn't know why, but she wanted to see him, not just to check if he had any suspicions, but also because she wanted to see if he was okay. Emotions and tensions had been high, and he didn't even acknowledge or look at her during the ceremony. At first, she thought it might have been because he had been preoccupied, but now, she wasn't sure. There was this tightness in her stomach that hadn't been there before, and now, worry nagged at her.

Scanning the room, she searched for him. She saw almost everyone else. Ben and Nate were talking to some high school friends at their table, Kate and Nikos raced to finish as many shots as they could by the bar, and Sybil and Riva were laughing with a group of other women. But, where was he?

Ah, there he was. She spotted the familiar, tall figure in the middle of the dance floor. When he swung around, that knot in her stomach grew even tighter.

Jason had his arms around another woman. The same brunette from the bar, she realized. The woman had her long, lean body pressed up against his, arms would tight, and the skirts of her red dress swished around them as they danced. He had his hand spread over her bare lower back and he dipped her low, twisting her body as she threw her head back and laughed.

Her blood pounded in her ears, and a knife-like pain stabbed her in the gut. She turned away, whipping around so she didn't have to watch that anymore.

"Christina," Sybil's voice broke through the clouded haze of her mind. "Thank God I've found you. Kate's been looking for you. Said she's going to drag you to the bar for some shots."

The idea sounded great right about now.

Sybil frowned when a high-pitched giggle rang over the din of the room. "Ugh," she said in a disgusted tone. "I can't believe Jason invited that ... person to be his date."

"Who?" she managed to choke out.

"Jessica What-ser-name," she sneered. "She's so crass. All she wants to talk about is how much this painting or that rug cost. I think I see dollar signs in her eyes. But it's not surprising with the caliber of women Jason hangs around with." She sighed. "Mom and I were talking. We were saying how we just wished he would settle down, you know? Someone nice. And classy. Like Catherine. Or you."

She let out a nervous laugh. "What?"

"I mean, not that I would wish the disaster that is my brother on you."

"Right." She cleared her throat. "Well, thanks for the heads-up on Kate. I think I'll go and powder my nose."

"No prob. I'll try to keep her distracted."

"Thanks." As Sybil strode back to the bar, Christina headed in the opposite direction. Where, she wasn't sure, but the atmosphere in the reception was choking her. The air suddenly felt hot and thick and she was dying for a breath of fresh air.

She managed to traverse the crowd of people and found the exit out into the anteroom. There were a few people lingering outside, and she quickly walked past them. She turned a few hallways, but realized she was lost. *Who the hell needed a thirty-room castle?*

Christina collected her thoughts, trying to figure out where the hell she was. Pivoting on her feet, she decided to trace her way back. As she made her way down the darkened hallways, the air suddenly grew cold. She stopped short and peered ahead at the looming shadow that was coming closer.

"Jason."

He walked toward her slowly, the sound of his shoes pounding on the hardwood floor echoing in her ears with each step. As he came closer, the single chandelier overhead lit his handsome face. He had discarded his coat and tie, and the top buttons of his shirt were open, exposing his tanned throat.

The hallway suddenly felt small as he towered over her. He had shaved that morning, the stubble gone from his jaw. His eyes glowed, like two silvery moons on a dark night. "Did you get lost?"

She let out the breath she didn't realize she'd been holding. "Yeah. Silly me, huh?"

He jerked his thumb behind him. "Front door's that way."

"Huh?"

"What? Isn't your hot deputy waiting for you now?"

What was he talking about? "Who?"

"Cole." Hatred dripped in his voice. "Isn't that why you were talking to him today?"

"Oh please," she said. "Don't even pretend you care."

He gripped her arm. "And don't you deny it. I overhead Kate and Sybil talking. They said you and the good deputy were going to get to know each other."

She tried to wrench away from him, but his grip was too strong. "It's not like that."

"Then what is it like?" He dragged her over to the wall and pushed her back up against one of the doors.

"None of your business!" she hissed. He was so big and broad, she couldn't even see around him. She wiggled to get free, but he wouldn't budge. "Besides," she said. "What about you and *your date?* Will you be *getting to know each other* more tonight?"

His eyes glimmered with danger. "Are you jealous?"

"What? I am not."

"I wanted to kill Cole when you were touching him," he whispered, his voice almost a growl. "I don't want you to touch him. I don't want you near any man but me."

"Jason—"

He cut her off with a savage kiss. She tried to resist his cruel lips, but when he pinned her lower body with his, his hardness pressing against her, she let out a moan. His tongue, warm and tasting of whiskey, slipped into her mouth and she melted against him. His mouth was rough, claiming, taking, and she feared he'd devour her until there was nothing left.

She should have pushed him away. Stopped the whole thing and ran. But no. She moved her hands behind her, fumbling for the knob, turning it so the door opened, and they tumbled inside the room.

Their mouths broke free of one another for a moment, but his strong arms caught her and brought her back to him. He walked her back, his mouth never leaving hers, until she bumped into something hard and solid.

Hands slipped down her back and under her, lifting her up and planting her on the surface behind her. He spread her legs so he could move between them. He looked down at her, the heat in his eyes setting fire to her core. His fingers reached behind her and began to unzip her dress, then shoved her top down, exposing her breasts to the cool air. He groaned then leaned down to draw a nipple into his mouth. The sensation of his tongue swirling around her hardened bud made her burn even more, and her panties flooded with the wetness that signaled her desire for him.

She fumbled at the buttons of his shirt and when she finally opened them all, pushed the fabric aside so she could feel him. The muscles under his hot, taut skin rippled as her hands touched him everywhere. God, had she ever wanted someone as much as she craved him? Never in her life.

He pulled away from her breasts, moving up her neck, then back to capture her mouth. This time, his kisses were drugging and slow, but just as passionate. She needed him so bad, and she reached down toward the front of his pants, moving her palm over his substantial erection.

"Jason!" she cried out when he shoved his hands under her skirt. His fingers found her lacy underwear, and ripped them to shreds, then pushed her skirt up to her waist. "Yes."

"Christina," he whispered against her mouth. "I didn't bring any protection."

"I'm safe," she said, drawing his zipper down. She'd been taking birth control since she was eighteen to control her terrible cramps. It was a good thing, because she didn't want to feel anything between them.

He shoved his pants and underwear down, his rock-hard cock jutting forward. She prayed she was wet enough to take him. Not that she cared. She needed him inside her now. "Please, Jason."

He growled, and pushed her legs further apart. She threw her head back, waiting, feeling the tip of his cock press against her folds. His shaft slid into her, slowly, letting her adjust to his girth. She rolled her hips, urging him on and caught his mouth in another desperate kiss.

He lifted the back of her knee, wrapping her leg around him as he shoved deeper into her. Inch by inch, stretching her, moving in until he was fully seated inside. It felt incredible, unlike any sensation she'd felt before.

Jason eased back halfway then pushed into her again. He repeated it, getting faster and faster each time. She let out an urgent noise with each thrust, which only seemed to spur him on.

An animalistic growl and a rumble emanated from deep in his chest and he buried his face in her neck, moving lower to suck on the flesh just above her breasts. She gasped at the slight pain of his teeth grazing her skin. The pain mixed with pleasure was too much and she grabbed onto his shoulders. He changed the angle of his hips, moving with shallow, short thrusts, hitting her clit just right with every stroke.

The pleasure was mind-numbing, and as he drove deeper into her, she cried out as an orgasm exploded through her. He didn't stop, pushing and driving faster. He throbbed inside of her—she could feel every pulse as his warmth filled her. She shuddered with a smaller orgasm, the wave of pleasure making her sex pulse as she milked him. He grunted with one final thrust then relaxed, his body pressing back into hers.

How long they stood like that, she wasn't sure. Her mind was still reeling at what they'd done. Her body felt boneless from the pleasure, and she let out a sigh.

His body froze and stiffened against her then he moved back, drawing out of her. The silence between them hung in the air. She didn't know what to say. Didn't know what he would say. But she didn't expect his next words.

"I'm sorry..." he rasped as he staggered back. "I can't."

The shock of his words held her immobile. He didn't even look at her; instead, he backed away as he righted himself. She was still staring at him, but not really seeing him or anything for that matter, as her vision darkened. He must have left because she distinctly heard the door close.

She didn't know how long she sat there. The numbness

that had spread through her seemed to have impaired her sense of time. She got off the table, pulled up her dress and let the skirt of her gown fall around her. She walked out of the room, following the path she had taken to get there, and back to the east wing to the guest room. She opened the door and crept in as quietly as she could.

"Christina?" a sleepy voice called from the bed.

"Cordy?"

Her sister sat up from the bed, rubbing her eyes. "Are you coming to bed?"

"Yes, I'm coming." She closed the door behind her. "I just need to change." She went to the bathroom and stripped off her gown, then stepped into the glass shower. Turning the knob, she let the hot water lash over her.

I'm sorry. I can't.

The emotions seemed to unfreeze as the scalding water hit her body. Anger and humiliation coursed through her. Anger for letting things go too far. Humiliation because despite what he said, her sex still pulsed with need for him even as she washed his seed from her thighs.

A cry ripped from her throat and she smothered a sob. No, she wouldn't weep for that bastard. She would never set foot in Blackstone for the rest of her life. She didn't care if she hardly saw Catherine, because the only way to get rid of the pain in her heart was to never see Jason Lennox ever again.

CHAPTER 13

"Get up."

The voice was muffled, like he was hearing it from under water.

"I said, get up."

The kick to his side wasn't particularly painful, but it was annoying. "Fuck off," Jason groused.

"It's almost noon, asshole." Luke's voice was much clearer now.

Light blinded his vision when he tried to open his eyes. He turned to his side. "Owww..." The pounding in his head was relentless. Jesus, he hadn't had a hangover since he was a teenager. It took a lot of alcohol to get a shifter wasted. "How much did I have to drink?" He sat up. Looking around, he saw that he was on Luke's couch in his cabin.

"Way too much." Luke sat down beside him and handed him a bottle of water.

Jason grabbed the bottle and chugged it in one go, letting the cool liquid quench his parched throat. He slammed the bottle down. "What happ—" The events of last night came flooding back in his mind. The wedding. The bomb. *Christina*.

Bitter jealousy had been boiling in him all day since he saw her approach Cole. He had been professional enough, but she had been flirting with him, giving him touches here and there. He tried to forget about it, even going as far as using Jessica as a distraction. Then he overheard Kate and Sybil talking about how Christina and Cole were going to get to know each other and the jealous rage took over. He saw her sneak out of the reception, and his imagination had gotten the best of him. Then he lost control and took what he wanted.

It was the most intense sexual experience of his life. Everything and everyone else faded away. And then his dragon spoke up.

Mine. Mate.

No.

His words came back to him. He didn't want a mate. He didn't deserve a mate. And he certainly didn't deserve Christina, not after what he did to her. Practically forced himself on her because of his jealousy. Lost control.

He told her he was sorry and walked out. He ran into Jessica, who had offered to go home with him, but he couldn't. Christina's sweet scent was still all over him, and he didn't want Jessica's stink anywhere near him. So he walked out, drove like mad to The Den and drank until he blacked out.

"Fuck." He slammed a fist on Luke's coffee table. "Did I do anything? Hurt anyone?"

Luke shook his head. "You didn't want to leave after closing. Tim called me."

He made a mental note to apologize to Tim. "You brought me here?" He looked around Luke's cabin. It was sparse, but clean. It was also in the middle of butt-fuck nowhere, deep in the mountains.

"You tore out of the reception without your wallet or house keys. Where the fuck else was I supposed to bring you?" Luke towered over him, staring him down with those golden eyes. "Now, are you going to tell me what's the matter?"

"What the hell do you care," he countered. "You're the one who pushed us away. You know. Your family."

"Don't make this about me," Luke growled. "I'm not the one trying to drink himself to death and acting like a damn fool."

"What do you know?"

"I know you haven't been the same since you met Christina. She's the one, isn't she? Your mate."

He opened his mouth to speak, but nothing came out. "Who told you?"

"You did."

Fucking asshole.

"What the hell happened between the two of you?" Luke asked.

"I don't need a damn mate." He was too ashamed to tell him what happened. That he took what he wanted and acted like a bastard afterwards. Because that was what he was. A pussy-chasing bastard who would just break her heart.

"You know, Jason, some of us aren't meant for mates. But you are."

"What the fuck are you talking about?"

Luke sat down next to him. "For someone who's always in tune with what others feel and want, you never once show your true feelings. You put on this playboy facade and pretend that you don't need anyone. Tell me, why do you screw all those women? What hole are you trying to fill inside you? What's been missing in your life?"

His brother's words rang over and over again in his ears. And then, it was like something in him answered.

Christina. That's what had been missing.

"Fuck." He turned to Luke. "When the hell did you start talking this much?"

He shrugged.

Jason shot to his feet. "I need to get back to the castle." He ran for the door then realized he probably didn't drive his truck here. "Shit."

Luke huffed. "I'll take you."

"Thanks, bro."

Luke grabbed his keys, and soon they were driving out of his property and making their way to Blackstone Castle. The engine had barely shut off before Jason raced to the front door. He threw it open, and nearly collided into Meg.

"Jason!" she exclaimed. "Where's the fire, young man?"

"Christina. Where is she?"

"She left," Meg said. "They all left for the airport about an hour ago. Matthew and Catherine for their honeymoon, Ari and his family back to Lykos."

Despair crept into him. Lykos was the Ari Stavros' secret island retreat. No one knew where it was. Once the plane took off, he wouldn't have any way to contact Christina. He supposed he could wait for two weeks when Catherine came back, so he could ask her how to contact Christina. That was, assuming his new sister-in-law would even talk to him when she found out what happened.

"Shit!" Meg raised a brow at him. "Er, sorry Meg," he apologized. "You can wash my mouth out with soap another time, okay?" He gave her a kiss on the cheek. "I'll see you later."

Jason sprinted back to the truck. He had to catch up to her now. "Airport," he said to Luke.

The regional airport where the Stavros private jet was parked was an hour away, but Luke made it in forty-five minutes. Luke drove right onto the runway, ignoring the guard screaming obscenities at them when his truck pummeled through the barrier. But the runway was empty and so was the hangar. They were too late.

"Dammit!" Jason slammed his palms on the dash. "Fuck!" He buried his face in his hands. The spark of hope he had that he'd get there in time had been extinguished. He'd lost her. She was perfect and his, and he drove her away.

A heavy hand landed on his shoulders. "Let's get you back home," Luke said. "Get you cleaned up."

The shower had felt refreshing, though it did nothing to get rid of the numbness that was creeping in. He had lost her. Over and over again, the words rang in his head.

His dragon was surprisingly quiet. Nothing—not a peep. Had it given up, too? Maybe they had truly lost Christina and now, only the hollow pain in his heart remained.

He didn't want to feel this way anymore. He drew the blackout curtains in his bedroom together then crept into bed. Fatigue seeped into his bones, and thankfully, the darkness of sleep took over.

Jason awoke with a jolt. Looking at the clock, he realized he had slept most of the day and night. It was already the next morning.

He padded out to his living room and much to his surprise, Luke was still there. "I thought you'd left," he said.

"Can't leave you when you're like this."

"Like what?" he asked.

Luke didn't answer, but instead, handed him his phone.

"What's this?"

"Only I know how to get in touch with Matthew," he said. Thanks to yesterday's events, Matthew and Catherine had cancelled their honeymoon in Paris, and instead, decided to go on a secret trip. No one knew where they were going for safety reasons.

"Matthew's going to kill me," he said.

"He'll understand." Luke shoved the phone at him. "Go."

He took a deep breath and accepted the phone with a grateful nod. He pressed the green button and put the receiver to his ear.

"This better be good," Matthew answered in an annoyed voice.

"It's me."

"Jason? What the—You left the reception without saying goodbye and no one could find you! If Luke hadn't called Dad … Where the hell have you been?"

"Getting my head outta my ass," he said wryly.

"Explain."

Jason let out a sigh. "Christina. You were right. She's the one. My mate. And now she's gone." He briefly explained what happened to Matthew. "It's my fault for driving her away. And I want her back."

Matthew sighed. "What can I do?"

"Let me talk to Catherine, please. I need some way to contact Christina. Before it's too late." *Before she hates me even more than she does now.*

"Of course."

There was a pause then he heard soft voices before Catherine came on the line. "Jason?"

"Catherine, please," he said. "You have to tell me how to get to Lykos. I need to see Christina."

"I'm sorry, Jason," Catherine said. "I can't tell you where Lykos is. I've been sworn to secrecy and I'll be putting hundreds of people in danger if I tell you."

"I'm not going to hurt anyone."

"Even if I did tell you, you'll never get there. There are no flights or public ferries to the island."

"I'm a dragon, remember?" He would fly for thousands of miles, if it meant seeing her again.

"Jason, Lykos has defenses you've never even heard of. They'll shoot you down before you even get a glimpse of the island."

Jason let out a frustrated sigh. "Then how can I contact her? Where is she based? Where's her office?"

"Er ... it's not like that. She's not strictly based in one place..."

"Please, Catherine. I'm begging you."

There was a pause. "Jason, I swear to God, if you hurt her again—"

"I won't. I love her." The words just came out with no warning. And he realized it was true.

Mine. Mate.

Catherine's breath hitched. "Really?"

"Yes, I really do. She's mine."

"Good," she said. "Look, Christina's ... job with Stavros involves a lot of travel. I spoke to her before they left, and she still wasn't sure where they were sending her next. All I know is that when she's done, she'll probably stop by our London townhouse. I can't tell you which day she'll arrive. It could be days or even weeks."

"Not a problem," Jason said. "Tell me where it is."

She rattled off the address, which he committed to memory. "Thanks Catherine, I owe you."

"You just go get your mate," she said wryly. "You know she's not going to come to you without a fight."

He smiled to himself. "That's why I love her." He thanked Catherine one last time before hanging up.

"Well?" Luke asked.

"I need to be on the first flight out to London."

CHAPTER 14

JASON PUT the two cups of coffee beside him as he sat down on the cold, concrete stoop. The bag of goodies was still warm on his lap. He planted his elbows on his knees and waited, watching the traffic on the now-familiar street in London's trendy Chelsea area.

"Excuse me, young man."

Jason looked up. An old woman wearing a thick, gray wool coat and matching hat was peering down at him. "What are you doing?"

"Waiting," he said. "I'm waiting."

"For what?" she asked, her wrinkled face tilting upward. "You were yesterday, too. Waiting on these steps for hours. I know because I've been watching you from my living room." She pointed to the house across the street.

"I'm waiting for someone."

"Oh?" Curious eyes stared at him. "Who?"

"A woman."

"Why?"

He let out a sigh. "I messed up. She's the best thing that ever happened to me, and I screwed it up."

"And now?"

"And now I'm going to do what it takes to win her back."

Her face lit up. "Whatever it takes?"

He nodded. "I'm going to beg for her forgiveness as soon as she comes home. Get down on my knees. Give her whatever she wants."

The woman sighed. "I was going to call the police," she said. "But now … I wish you luck, young man." She turned around and toddled back to her house.

Sitting there in the cold for the second day in row, Jason wondered if he should have thought this through first. He had been high on emotions when he booked the first ticket he could to Heathrow. He'd barely slept on the flight.

It was a good thing his parents were still in Blackstone. His mother had agreed to interrupt their around the world trip so she could step in and manage the day-to-day operations at Lennox Corp. while Matthew was on his honeymoon. Jason explained to them where he was going and his father hadn't even hesitated when he asked him to take over Lennox Foundation again, as well as his duties at the mines. His parents were elated that he had found his mate. He only hoped that he wouldn't disappoint them if he failed to bring Christina back to Blackstone. No—failure was not an option.

What was his plan, exactly? What would she say to him? What would *he* say to her? He tried to run the scenarios in his head, but he came up blank.

He stayed on her stoop until it was dark, late into the night. By the time it was midnight, it was time to go back to his hotel and get some sleep, then start the wait all over again.

The next day, he sat on the stoop again. By afternoon, the

lady from across the street, Mrs. Watson, came up to him again, this time, bringing a thermos of hot tea. The day after that, she invited him to her home, but he declined. He didn't want to miss Christina if she arrived that day.

By the fifth day, he was beginning to wonder if she'd even show up at all. It had also started to rain by lunch time, and he once again declined Mrs. Watson's invitation. He remained in his spot, letting the cold raindrops pelt him as he waited.

CHAPTER 15

CHRISTINA WINCED as she touched her side. *That's going to bruise.* She shifted in her seat, hoping no one would notice. The cabin of their plane was crowded with other agents and she had chosen the seat in the farthest corner. At least the mission had been successful, and they were now on their way back to Lykos for their debrief.

"That guy got you good," Kostas said as he sat down on the empty seat next to her. "You're going to have a nasty bruise."

"Thanks for letting me know, Sherlock," she said sarcastically.

Kostas' face turned serious. "Christina, what's wrong with you?"

"What do you mean?"

"Your head's not here. If you're not staring into space, you're moody and snappish," he said. "And that guy clocking you? Rookie mistake. You were wide open and that's not what we taught you."

"I'm fine," she insisted. "I'm just worried."

"I know," Kostas said. "We still have no lead on the bomb. Intelligence will be ready to break into Blackstone P.D.'s servers once they have their final report. We'll find out whoever planted it. But, we've still got other cases."

"Don't you think I know that?" she snapped. Kostas shot her a look. Okay, so she was proving his point.

"It's been a hard few days," he said. "You've had almost no downtime since the wedding. I told you we didn't need you here. It's a standard infiltration op."

"I wasn't tired," she said. "And I needed to get back to work." She needed the distraction or else her emotions would have eaten her right up.

"Well, now you're going to get some downtime until you get your head on straight." She tried to protest but he held his hand up. "Don't make me tell Papa or Xander. You know they can order you to get rest or even put you on desk duty."

She huffed. Her father was just waiting for an excuse to get her out of the field. "Fine," she relented. "I'll head to London for a few days." She hated London—the throngs of tourists, the noise, the pollution—but it would mean that she'd be close to Cordy. She could wait until the weekend then take her sister out of school. They could have a girls' day in SoHo. "I'll take the first flight I can after the debrief."

"Good."

Christina reclined her seat and struggled to find a comfortable position as she put her blanket over her head. Even though the cabin was quiet and she had her eye mask on, sleep eluded her, as it had for days.

Each time she closed her eyes, the memories of that night came flooding back. *I'm sorry. I can't.* She thought that saying it over and over again would make it hurt less each time, but it was the opposite. The more she thought about it ... well, she didn't want to think about it anymore. She didn't want to think about Jason. That's why she'd left Blackstone as soon as she could, so she could forget. But her traitorous mind wouldn't let her, and it kept playing the events in her head. Jason's kisses. His hands. Making love. The most intense orgasm of her life. And then his words.

I'm sorry. I can't.

No. She refused to cry over him. That bastard. He wanted one thing, and when he got it, he dropped her.

Never again. She was never going to open herself up to that kind of hurt again. She had forgotten her purpose while she was in Blackstone. From now on, she would only focus on fighting the cruelty and evil in the world. She tugged the blanket closer around her, willing her tired mind to sleep.

The flight to London was short and went by in a blur. She had left only a few hours after the debrief. Though she wanted to stay a bit longer, she couldn't stand the suspicious looks her brothers had been giving her. They knew something was up, and trying to hide anything from them would be like trying to take a bone away from a hungry dog. And so she thought a few days away from them would help her recalibrate.

As the black cab drove through the streets of London, she stared blankly outside the window, watching the scenery pass by and the rain fall from the sky. This was the land of her birth, of her mother's family, but she felt no connection here. It seemed strange and the memories of growing up in this city were faded in her mind. Lykos was her home and being in this dank, gloomy city only solidified that.

The cab stopped in front of the townhouse and she

thanked the driver as she handed him a few bills. She stepped out, overnight bag in one hand, and made her way to the front steps. It hadn't stopped raining since she landed, and she didn't have an umbrella, but it was only a few feet to the front door. She fished for her keys in her purse, her mind so preoccupied that she didn't notice the figure sitting on the steps until she was nearly on top of him. She blinked.

"Jason?"

The dark head looked up. His face was blank, almost like he couldn't believe he was looking at her. Then, the silvery-gray eyes flashed and his expression turned to relief. He shot to his feet.

She should have slapped him. Railed at him. Told him to go to hell. But no. She stood there, doing and saying nothing as shock made its way through her system.

They stood there for a minute, looking at each other in the rain and cold. How long had he been waiting here? His hair was damp and his shirt was so soaked through that the fabric clung to his chest. Her mouth went dry, thinking of his hot, naked body.

"Christina," he said, his voice raspy. "I'm sor—"

She cut him off. "Don't you dare say those words to me."

"I'll never apologize for anything again, if it'll make you happy."

His words boggled her and she didn't know what to say, so she sputtered out the first thought in her head. "How long have you been waiting here?"

"How long today?"

"Today?"

"I left Blackstone the day after you did, as soon as Catherine gave me the address," he confessed. "I didn't know when you'd get here, so I've been waiting every day. Christina, I just want to talk."

"Right." Talk. That was all he wanted to do. He came across the pond, waiting here for days, just to talk to her. "It's raining out here." She walked past him, jogged up the steps and slipped her key into the door. "We should go inside. To talk."

CHAPTER 16

JASON FOLLOWED Christina into the townhouse, still stunned. She stepped aside to let him in then closed the door behind them.

Frankly, he was surprised that she had let him in. Or that she was talking to him. The moment he heard his name on her lips, the hope he thought had died bloomed again. Now, he had to convince her to be with him. To be his mate forever. That morning, he finally found the words he wanted to say to her and he was ready.

"Christina," he began. Her back was still turned to him and he heard the lock click in place. "I wanted to talk so—"

She whipped around. "I don't want to talk, Jason."

"Oh." What now? Should he beg on his knees for her forgiveness? Leave her alone and never see her again?

Christina took a step forward and placed her hands on his chest. "I said, I don't want to *talk*." She got on her tiptoes then pulled him down for a kiss.

The soft touch of her lips was a delicious sensation and for a moment, he thought he was hallucinating, that this was all a dream and he was going to wake up alone. But no, she was definitely real. The hands tugging at his shirt was real. Her lips were warm and real. And when he realized just how real she was, he grabbed her waist and pulled her to him.

The touch of their bodies made her sigh against his mouth and he realized he couldn't wait anymore. He picked her up in her arms. "Bedroom?" he asked.

"Upstairs, first door on the right."

He took the steps two at a time, carrying her up all the way. Unable to wait, he kicked the door down, causing her to giggle. He approached the bed and lay her down on top of the soft covers.

"I can't believe you're here," she said, touching his face.

He turned his head and kissed her palm. "I didn't want you to leave. I—"

"Make love to me again," she said.

Her words brought a surge of desire through him and he wanted nothing more than to do exactly as she said. He removed her top reverently, taking his time, exposing her sweet, creamy flesh to his gaze. The last time had been quick and urgent, and he didn't have time to admire her beautiful body. Now, he was going to savor every inch of her.

"What the hell?" he frowned at a burgeoning a bruise on her side. "What the fuck happened? Who hurt you?"

"It's nothing," she said, reaching for him. "Kickboxing class. My partner got sloppy and hit me." She grabbed his hands and pulled him to her. "Don't stop now..."

He nodded then moved between her legs, pulling her pants down and tossed them over his shoulder. The white cotton panties she was wearing had a wet spot in front, and he leaned down to lick it, tasting and smelling her desire.

"Jason," she cried out.

Pulling her panties down, his eyes devoured her wet, pink pussy. She was incredible. He couldn't help himself and he dove right in.

Her thighs pressing on his ears muffled her cries, but based on the way she was thrusting her hips up, she was definitely enjoying herself. He was too, licking up the delicious wetness of her cunt, sliding into her tight passage, and feeling her clench around his tongue.

He slid a finger into her, while he moved his mouth up to her clit. His lips clamped onto the sensitive bud, and she *really* enjoyed that. Her hips bucked up, wanting more and he gladly gave it to her. He sucked on her clit and fucked her with his fingers until she was shaking with her orgasm.

"Please, no more," she begged, her breath labored.

"I'm not done," he said. "I'll never be done." He pressed his mouth to her and coaxed another orgasm, making her back arch off the bed and her hands twist the sheets into knots.

When she recovered, she sat up and dragged him over her body, her eyes blazing with lust. "Get inside me. Now."

He couldn't deny her what she wanted. "Yes, ma'am," he said with a cheeky grin. "But you might regret it."

She raised her brow at him. "Why?"

"Because I won't stop until you come for me over and over again," he said, pulling her ankles around his waist. He was already hard and ready, and he guided his cock to her entrance. God, he loved the feel of her raw against him. He was glad she was on birth control, but he'd have to insist she stop taking it from now on. The thought of accidentally fathering children had always brought him into a cold sweat, but with Christina, he relished it.

He moved into her, slowly. She was still slick, but he was

big and the last time she needed more time to adjust. Christina eagerly moved her hips up to meet him, and he sank into her with a satisfied groan.

He waited for her muscles to relax around him, and when she pulled him down for a kiss, he began to move his hips. Slow, lazy thrusts at first, just to enjoy the feel of her clenching around him. When she began to hum with need, he moved faster, deeper, and reached down to stroke her clit with his fingers. Her first orgasm was quick, and she clawed her nails down his back, making him nearly come from the sensation. But, he gritted his teeth and held onto his control.

He pulled out, and she relaxed and sighed, but he was far from done. Grabbing her ankles, he twisted her around in one motion so she was on her knees.

She cried out in surprise and he surged into her again. He pulled her to him, pressing her back against his chest as he thrust into her over and over. Quick, hard, and deep. His hands reached around to cup her luscious tits, rolling her hard nipples between his fingers.

Her cries became louder, and she yelped with each thrust into her. He pushed her down, driving her forward on her knees until she was braced against the headboard. He pummeled into her relentlessly, not stopping until she had two more orgasms.

"Jason," she panted. "Come inside me."

Fuuuck, her dirty talk was a turn-on. He flipped her over again, and hauled her back by her ankles. He surged into her, pushing in deep then pulled back before thrusting into her again.

"Keep your eyes open and look at me," he said. Blue orbs opened wide, and stared up at him. "Beautiful," he whispered, stroking her cheek. He began to move again, short quick strokes that had her sighing and sinking her teeth into her luscious lower lip. He changed the angle so he could hit her clit just right and she clenched around him, shuddering in another orgasm. Satisfied, he moved faster, enjoying the feel of her slick, tight pussy around him, squeezing him.

He grunted and his balls clenched, and finally he let himself go. Waves of pleasure shot down his spine as he had one of the most intense orgasms in his life. His hips jerked a few more times, pumping her full of his cum. Just like she wanted.

Jason braced himself on his elbows so as not to crush her, and after he took a few seconds to collect himself, slipped out of her then rolled them over so she was on top. Christina let out a contented sigh and relaxed against him and he wrapped his arms around her.

The air cooled around them, the hum of the A/C the only sound in the room. Christina's body grew heavier, and as he looked down, he saw her eyes closed, her calm and peaceful face, her golden hair spread over his chest. It reminded him of that first time they slept together like this. Satisfied, he closed his own eyes, letting sleep take over.

Jason woke up fully aware of where he was. In fact, his mind had never been more clear in his life. Making Christina his mate was the one thing he was sure he wanted. And he couldn't wait until it was official. But how did this work? He wished he'd paid more attention to his dad when he'd explained it. Well, Hank never explained how the mating process worked exactly. All he told them was that they would know it the moment it happened.

He reached over, finding the space next to him empty. He sat up, scratching his head. Where was she? They had been entwined the whole afternoon and evening, making love through the morning. He made her come over and over again, as he threatened. She begged him to stop, but he ignored her. Christina coming was one of the most intensely beautiful things he'd ever seen. Watching her sleep was the second, and he only let her close her eyes because he wanted to stare at her peaceful face while she slumbered.

He got up and picked up his discarded pants, hopping into them as he walked out of the bedroom. He glanced around, but couldn't find his shirt. He thought he had placed it on the heater sometime during the night to dry it out. Where was it? Not that it mattered. He wasn't planning on leaving anytime soon.

There was noise coming from downstairs, and he followed the sound. He turned right at the bottom of the stairs, to what he assumed was the kitchen. Sure enough, Christina was there, back to him, humming softly to herself as she stood by the stove, wearing nothing but his shirt.

He smiled and leaned against the doorway. "I could get used to this."

Christina turned around, and she flashed him a smile. "I'm making breakfast. Bacon and eggs?"

"Yes, please," he said. She motioned for him to sit down at the counter where she'd set up two place settings, then put some scrambled eggs and crispy bacon on his plate.

He took a bite of the bacon and she turned to the stove, but before she could walk away, he grabbed her hand and pulled her back so she straddled him.

"Hey," she said, settling onto his lap.

"Hey," he answered then gave her a quick kiss on the lips. "So ... about that talk."

Her mouth twisted. "I said I don't want to talk."

"Christina…"

She rocked against his hips, grinding against him. He groaned as he suddenly became hard from the friction and heat of her pussy through his pants. "Looks like someone doesn't want to talk, either."

"Christina," he warned.

She gave him a seductive smile then slid off his lap. "I think he'd rather be doing something else." She reached down between his legs and popped the buttons on his fly, releasing his cock. He was already half hard, but she made quick work of him as she stroked and pumped his shaft. He could see the desire clouding her eyes, right before she leaned down to take him in her mouth.

"Jesus." His hands gripped the counter, the sensation of her wet mouth around him too much. "Christina." His fingers shoved into her hair, guiding her gently. She slid her mouth along his length expertly, her tongue doing delicious things to him. Mouthing him enthusiastically, she looked at him, her blue eyes staring into his as his shaft slid between her luscious lips. She closed her eyes and let out a long moan.

It was too much. The sight of her on her knees. His cock in her mouth. The feel of her tongue and lips. "God ... baby ... you can't ... " He tried to tug her up, but she pushed his hands away. Deciding to let her have her way, he gripped her by the hair and thrust his hips into her mouth.

"I ... ugh ... " He let out a pleasured grunt, feeling his balls tighten and then release into her mouth. She wouldn't even let him pull out, instead, drinking up every drop of cum from his cock.

He sat there in a daze, his cock still pulsing as she pulled her mouth away. His blood was still ringing in his ears when Christina stood up and wiped her mouth with the back of her hand. "Hmmm ... I enjoyed breakfast. Did you?"

Hot damn.

CHAPTER 17

THEY SPENT the whole day in bed, never leaving unless absolutely necessary. Jason couldn't get enough of Christina, but he had this sinking feeling that she was avoiding him. Well, not *him*, but whenever he wanted to talk, she either changed the subject or did something sexy that made him forget what he was trying to say. He didn't want to think it was deliberate, but after the third or fourth attempt, he was definitely getting suspicious. It was frustrating, but he was determined to get through to her. That's why he suggested going out to dinner that night. Surely, she wouldn't try anything in public.

"Out?" she asked, turning her head to look back at him. "Why would you want to go out?" She was getting out of bed to go to the bathroom, fully naked. He tried to not let her delectable heart-shaped ass distract him from his mission.

"To eat," he said. "And maybe you can show me around a bit. This is my first time in London, and I've only seen the outside of your house and the inside of your bedroom. There must be some good restaurants around."

She shrugged. "Fine. I know a couple of places."

They weren't far from the trendy shopping area with shops, cafes and restaurants. There were about half a dozen quiet, romantic restaurants where they could have had dinner, but she took him to a noisy pub. On the night that two rival football teams were having a game.

"Do you want a beer?" Jason shouted over the din of football fans at the bar, howling in delight as their team scored.

"What?" she yelled back, cupping her palm to her ear. "What's wrong with my hair?"

"I said, do you want a beer?" He pointed to the bar and she nodded.

As they sat at their table and ate, alternately screaming and making hand gestures at each other, that sinking suspicion grew bigger. But he wasn't going to give up. At the end of the night after he paid for their dinner, he insisted on walking back to the town house instead of taking a cab.

They walked in silence most of the way, but as soon as they got to the building, Jason knew it was now or never. They were standing in front of the stoop and he grabbed her hand to bring her to a halt.

"What is it?" she asked.

"You've been avoiding talking to me. Don't deny it," he said before she could protest. "We need to talk."

"Can't we go back inside first?" she asked, tracing her fingers on his chest and looking up at him seductively.

"No," he said firmly. "Don't think I didn't notice that you keep trying to distract me with sex. Now, unless you want to put on a show for Mrs. Watson," he jerked his thumb at the house across the street, "you're going to listen to what I have to say."

"There's nothing to talk about," she sulked, crossing her arms over her chest.

"Nothing to talk about?" he asked in an incredulous voice. What was the matter with her? "I came all the way here to find you, to be with you, and you don't want to hear what I have to say?" He gripped her arms. "Christina, you're my ma—"

Pain ripped through his arm before he could finish his sentence. He blinked and looked down. Blood dripped down his bicep through a hole in his shirt. Alarm bells began to ring in his head. "Inside!" he shouted, dragging her up the steps. More bullets whizzed by and another caught him in the thigh. He ignored the burning pain and kicked the door down, then pushed them both inside.

"Go out the back door," he ordered. "And get far away."

"No!" she said, her eyes growing in horror. "I won't leave you."

"Christina, you need—"

Before he could tell her to leave again, the door crashed open. Boots stomped on the ground and as he turned around, several red dots appeared on his and Christina's chest. He lifted his head slowly.

It was dark inside the townhouse, but his eyes adjusted quickly. There were six men in black combat gear and Kevlar armor surrounding them, weapons trained on them both. They were wearing full head and face armor, so he couldn't see what they looked like.

"Who are you?" he shouted. His dragon was screaming to get out, to turn these men who dared to threaten him and his mate to ashes. But he couldn't risk it. He'd survive, but Christina wouldn't. Their automatic weapons would pump her body full of bullets before he finished shifting. "What do you want?" The men remained silent, unmoving.

"We're not here for you," a voice said. A light flickered on inside the house, and the six men shuffled aside to let someone forward.

The man wore similar gear to the others, but he wasn't wearing a helmet or mask. He was tall and built like a brick wall and his confident air told Jason he was their leader. His weathered face might have been handsome once, but the numerous scars across his face marred his features. His white hair was cropped close to his scalp, military-style. Steely eyes stared right at him. "Don't try anything funny, Blackstone dragon," he said. "Or she gets it." He raised a hand and the dots zeroed in on Christina's forehead.

"So you know who I am," Jason said. "And what I'm capable of. If you kill her, I'm going to burn every single one of you until there's nothing left."

The man's mouth twisted into a cruel smile. "But then, she will still be dead," he said. "Care to try and see what happens?"

Jason cursed inwardly, but he remained calm. They wanted *something*, which is why they hadn't killed them yet. "So, what do you want?"

"Her," he said, nodding at Christina.

"No," he said flatly. "I'll come with you willingly. Just let her go."

"Didn't you hear what I said, dragon?" The man spat. "I don't want you. I want her."

"What the fuck for?"

"I'll come with you," Christina said. "Just don't hurt him."

"Fuck, no!" Jason pulled Christina behind him. "Why the hell do you want her? She's no one."

The man let out a sardonic laugh. "You don't know who she is, do you?"

What the hell was he saying? He looked to Christina, hoping for an explanation, but she remained silent, her expression inscrutable.

"We're finally going to get you, traitor," the man said. "Maybe your 'father' will trade you for something good. Or we could just keep you and punish you for your sins."

"What are you talking about?" Jason asked. "She's no traitor."

"She's a traitor to *my* kind!" The man stepped forward, reaching for Christina, but Jason stepped in front of him. He ignored him, and continued. "She's a human, but she chose to associate with your filthy kind. Living among wolf shifters as if she was one of them, and now, screwing a dragon. Disgusting," he sneered. He turned to Jason. "Your family wasn't supposed to be part of this. And then your brother decided to mate with her whore of a sister. Tell me, did they like our little wedding present?"

Rage filled Jason's veins. "You're responsible for that bomb."

"It was perfect. The accidents at the mines were supposed to distract you from our real target. All your security was focused on the mines and we hid the package right under your very noses. We would not only stop the joining together of two powerful shifter groups, but get rid of all of the Blackstone dragons and the Lykos Alpha and his sons." He let out an angry hiss. "But then you somehow foiled our plans." He looked back at Christina. "We should have killed you when you were a child. Just like when we killed your traitor whore mother. Too bad her repulsive child survived. But, we'll get her too."

"No!" Christina pushed Jason aside and lunged at the man. "You monster!"

Jason tried to stop her, but she moved too quickly. The

man grabbed her hands and then twisted her around, slamming her down to her knees. She cried out in pain.

"Bastard!" Jason bellowed. "You're dead!" His dragon was taking over, and he was only happy to let it.

"Get her to the van!" the man shouted, tossing Christina to one of the men. "And fire at will!"

Jason had never shifted so quickly before, but he knew Christina's life was on the line. The sounds of the automatic weapons firing was deafening, but the bullets ricocheted off his scales. His body grew to its full height, the roof and walls collapsing around him as his massive head hit the ceiling, crushing several of the men as the townhouse crumbled in a heap around him.

He let out an earth-shaking roar as he shook the debris off his head. *Christina.* They took her, meaning they wanted her alive, for now at least. But he would make sure they weren't going to touch a hair on her head.

His dragon wanted to burn everything down, but Jason knew he had to be in control. They weren't in the mountains and he couldn't just stomp around and spew fire when there were a dozen houses on this street alone. No matter how much he wanted to get those men, he was not going to harm any innocent people.

He turned his head at the sound of screeching tires and saw two vans speeding away. There wasn't a lot of space to stretch his wings, so he stomped after the vans, the ground shaking with each step. He caught the first one, carefully ripping the top with his claw to check if Christina was there. However, only the driver and one other man were in it. He tossed it aside with an angry huff, the other van nowhere in sight. He had wasted his time, and now they were going to get away with Christina. With a determined roar, he stomped down the street toward the direction of the other van.

Ah, there it was. They were maybe a mile away, and while it was difficult to run at full speed, he could catch up with his massive stride. He was almost there, a breath away when the van suddenly swerved, turned into an alleyway, then crashed into the wall. The back of the van opened, and he saw a small figure jump out.

Christina! She was alive! He had to get her out of there. But the alleyway was too small, and there was no way he was going to fit unless he tore the surrounding buildings down.

He roared to get her attention. She looked up, her eyes going wide as she saw him, then began running toward him. *Faster,* he urged her silently. He stepped back, getting ready to fly them off if needed. But, she only got a few feet away before she reared back. Three of the men had chased after her, and one of them grabbed her by the hair.

NO!

His dragon screeched with fury, clawing at the buildings to try and get to her, wings flapping wildly. Jason struggled to get the dragon under control. He looked down, hoping to God those men weren't hurting her, when he suddenly stopped.

He expected to see a kicking and screaming Christina being dragged away by the three men. Instead, Christina was kicking ass. The man who had grabbed her hair was already on the ground, clutching his stomach. The second man dove toward her, but she caught his hand and flipped him over, his back landing on the ground with a thud. Meanwhile, the third man was approaching her, handgun ready and drawn. She didn't even panic; instead, she disarmed him with a swipe of her hand, drew her knee up into his groin, and twisted him around. The sickening sound of breaking bones and the screams of pain filled the air.

What. The. Fuck.

Jason took over control of his body, pushing the dragon deep inside him, his body growing smaller and the scales receding into his skin. As soon as he was fully human, he bolted to her then embraced her.

"I thought I'd lost you," he whispered into her hair. "What the hell was that about?"

"There's no time to explain," she said, pulling away from him. She gasped when she saw the wounds on his thigh and arm.

"Shit." His arm was okay, but the blood was still pouring out of the wound on his thigh. "Bullet's still in that one."

"The police are almost here," she said, as the sounds of sirens rang through the air. "We need to go. Can you walk?"

He nodded. "Where are we going?"

"To a safe house. The nearest one's a few blocks away. Can you make it?"

The sirens were getting closer. "Yeah, I'll make it."

"Good." She grabbed his hand and took him to the other end of the alley, which led to another street. They got away just in time because the blue and red lights of the police car filled the darkened alleyway as they turned the corner.

He followed her, thankful for the darkness of night to cover their presence, not to mention his nakedness. Finally, they reached a nondescript apartment building four streets over from where they had started. They went around to the back, and Christina pulled a key ring from inside a hollowed-out brick beside the door. It swung open with a loud creak and they entered, going up two flights. When they reached the second floor, she led him to the first door on the left.

"Go in there," she said, pointing toward the bedroom. He limped inside then sat down on the lone futon in the room. Christina came in shortly with a first aid kit in hand and knelt in front of him. "This is going to hurt."

"Do it," he said through gritted teeth. He gripped the edge of the futon, waiting for the pain as she dug into the wound with a pair of tweezers. Finally, he let out his breath when he felt the bullet dislodge from his thigh.

She finished cleaning his wound, then turned back to grab something from the first-aid kit. It was a small bottle of clear liquid.

"I don't need that," he said. "My shifter healing will fight off any infection."

"I know," she said in a quiet voice. Something glinted in her hand. A long, silver needle. "This isn't for infection." Before he could ask her anything, she jabbed the needle into his thigh.

"What the fuck?"

"I'm sorry," she said, looking up at him. "I'm so sorry."

The last thing he remembered before the world went black was her beautiful face and the two tears that streaked down her cheeks.

CHAPTER 18

THE POUNDING at the door woke her. Christina quickly sat up, looked around, then let out a breath. She was safe. At least for now. She got up from the couch, dashed to the door and checked the keyhole.

"Kostas," she said as she opened the door and let him in. "Thank God you're here." She had used the laptop in the safe house to send an SOS back to HQ.

"Have you seen the news?" he said, after giving her a quick hug. "Someone got some grainy footage of a *dragon* stomping around Chelsea. We're working to get it off the Internet and control the story, but Father and Xander are going insane. Now tell me what happened."

"I don't know where to start."

"Then start at the beginning."

"Jason and I were attacked on the way home from dinner last night. They tried to kill us and so he didn't have a choice."

"Jason? *Lennox?*" Kostas raised a dark brow at her. "What was he doing there?"

"Does it matter?" she countered. "Anyway, that's not important. Those men—"

"Christina."

Coldness swept over her when she heard the raspy voice. Her head turned slowly toward the bedroom door.

Jason stood there, hand braced on the jamb, wearing the spare set of clothes she had laid out for him. His face was drawn into a fierce scowl, his silvery eyes glowing inhumanly. "You drugged me."

"I had no choice." He wasn't supposed to wake up now. She had timed it so she would be gone by the time he came to. That tranquilizer was formulated to knock out a shifter for a full twelve hours. Obviously, it wasn't enough for a dragon.

"No choice?" he staggered into the living room. When he tried to grab her, Kostas stood between them.

"Don't you dare, dragon," Kostas warned. His eyes flickered with power and the air in the room began to feel thin. "Do you know what you've done? How much trouble you caused?"

"Was I supposed to let those men take her?" he countered. "Who were they?" He looked at Christina. "Who are you?"

Christina's shoulders sagged. "Kostas," she said. "Can you give us some privacy?"

"I'm not leaving," her brother said.

"Please," she begged. "I'll be right out. I need to talk to Jason alone."

"Are you going to tell him—"

"He's already seen too much." Her eyes flickered back to Jason. "Please."

Kostas' jaw hardened. "Fine. But I won't be far away." With a last warning look at Jason, Kostas left, slamming the door behind him.

She looked back at Jason, who was pinning her to the spot with his gaze.

"Well?" he asked.

She took a deep breath. "I don't work for Stavros International's marketing department. I'm part of a secret agency my father established to protect shifters. We call ourselves the Shifter Protection Agency. It's not an official organization or anything. We don't exist. Stavros funds us through a dozen shell companies."

"What do you do?" he asked.

"Like I said, we protect shifters. We stop people like that man from last night."

"So you trained to fight?" he asked.

She nodded. "My brothers have been teaching me to defend myself since I was young. But, I only joined The Agency a year ago."

"Those men, they were after you because you worked for this agency?"

"Yes."

He shook his head. "I don't understand. We got away. You're safe. Why did you drug me?"

She swallowed the growing lump in her throat. It had been an impulse move. After what had happened, she panicked. She reasoned that she was doing it to protect The Agency, and to protect him. But, when she searched his eyes and saw the glimmer of anger there, it was obvious he knew why. Her silence said it all.

"You were going to run away from me again," he said, his voice like hard shards of glass piercing into her chest. "You were going to leave me and disappear. Without any explanation. Without letting me say what I came here to say."

"No," she denied, but the lie rang hollow in her own ears.

"I ... I can't do this!" Hands fisted at her sides. "Please, I have to go. The trail will be running cold and I have to get to work."

"Christina." He closed the distance between them in two steps. He pushed her back against the wall. "You're mine. You're my mate and you know it. My dragon knows it. And there's this legend—"

She pushed against him. "Who cares about your stupid family legend?"

Shock registered on his face. "You knew."

"So did you," she countered. "From the beginning, you knew I could tell you apart from Matthew and you said *nothing*. Did nothing."

"Don't put this on me," he said. "You could have told me all this time."

"What does it matter? And what do you want from me?"

"I want you to be my mate. Be with me forever."

She scoffed. "Live with you back in Blackstone? And then what? Wait until you get tired of me and you go back to Jessica or whoever catches your fancy next?"

He slammed his hands on the wall behind her, the force so hard his palms left dents in the drywall. "Stop it! You know what mating means. I'll only want you from now on. My dragon and I will be devoted to you for the rest of our lives. I couldn't go after anyone else, not even if I wanted to. Please, come back with me."

God, she wanted nothing more than to say yes, but it was all too much. His presence, her emotions, everything was threatening to take her over. "I can't."

"Why the hell not?" His eyes blazed with fury, and the air became choking cold. "You feel the same way, I know it."

"It doesn't matter what I feel. I can't go back to Blackstone with you. Not after yesterday."

"I'll protect you," he said. "I'll never let anyone harm you."

She hardened her heart. "Those *murderers* are still out there. After searching for them for sixteen years, we finally know where they are. I can't stop now, not when I can avenge Mama."

"But—"

"I can't, Jason." She turned her head, refusing to look at him. Because the pain in his eyes was too much and she might give in.

"Please, Christina. Don't do this."

"I have to." She ducked under his arms. Her legs felt like lead, and it was difficult, but she used every ounce of her strength to walk away from him. She thought he would go after her, but he didn't move. Didn't even make a sound when she left.

When she closed the door behind her, Kostas was waiting there, a puzzled look on his face. Before he could say anything, she put up her hand. "Don't. We have to go back to Lykos. We have work to do."

Though he looked like he had a million questions to ask her, Kostas simply nodded. "The jet is waiting."

The ride to the airstrip was silent, and Christina was glad Kostas didn't ask any questions about last night or about Jason. When they reached the private airstrip outside London, Kostas drove the car right up to the tarmac. The jet waiting was emblazoned with Stavros International's white and blue logo.

Christina walked up the stairs and with a heavy sigh, walked into the cabin. The heaviness in her chest seemed to grow with each step. *Stop it.* She was doing the right thing. She had to avenge Mama and protect Cordy. She didn't have time for a mate or for love.

The word struck her like lightning. Love? Had she fallen in love with Jason? Did he love her? He kept saying she was his and they were mates, yet she never heard that word from his lips.

Someone clearing his throat jolted her out of her thoughts. "Papa? Xander?" She had been so consumed by her thoughts that she didn't see the two men sitting on the white leather seats inside the cabin. Kostas walked up beside her, and she flashed him a dirty look. "You didn't tell me they were here, too."

"You didn't ask."

"Sit down, Christina," Ari Stavros said to his stepdaughter, pointing to the seat next to him. "We're about to take off."

She took her seat beside him and buckled the seatbelt, as did Kostas. The plane took off and Christina sat in tense silence, waiting for the hammer to fall. When the jet arrived at cruising altitude and the fasten seatbelt lights turned off, the flight steward appeared from the rear cabin to take their drink orders. Ari dismissed him with a wave of his hand.

"Now," Ari began when they were finally alone. "Explain what happened."

Three pairs of eyes looked at her. "It was them, Papa. They did it," she managed to choke out.

"Who?" Ari asked. "And what did they do?"

Christina rigidly held her tears in check and took a long, deep breath and began to relay what happened and what the man had said. "He confessed to killing Mama and hurting Cordy," she said at the end of her story.

Ari's eyes glowed with dazzling fury and he shot to his feet. "Who were they? DARSA? SPHK? Humans First?"

"I don't know," she answered. "He didn't say."

Ari turned to his sons and they looked at each other. He sat down and ran a hand through his hair.

"What?" she asked. "What's going on?"

The three men remained silent. Then, Xander spoke. "We've made some headway into the investigation surrounding the incidents in Blackstone."

"None of the usual anti-shifter groups are connected," Kostas continued. "Well, not directly. Someone's covering their tracks, and they hid it well."

"Is it a new group?" she asked.

Ari shook his head. "We don't know, but … this is big."

Kostas cleared his throat. "Using the report from Blackstone P.D., Intelligence followed a trail that led to an underground TOR network. First they only found the usual anti-shifter hate speech and propaganda. But, after digging deeper, we uncovered something else."

"A bigger group, possibly bigger than all the known anti-shifter organizations combined," Xander added.

"Larger than us, that's for sure," Ari said. "The amount of resources they have, the manpower, the cash … We don't know how we can take them on."

She gasped. "No." A group more powerful than Stavros and The Agency? "But Mama…"

"We'll get them," Ari vowed. "For what they did to her and Cordelia, and all our kind they hurt."

"They're definitely on to us," Xander said. "We'll have to be even more careful."

"We have to expand," Kostas said. "Bring in more recruits. Get more allies on our side. Our pack can't be the only one in this fight."

"No," Xander countered. "We can't work in secret if too many people know about us. We'd be putting everyone in Lykos in danger."

"But we'll never find them on our own!"

"We'll find a way, we always have. We don't need help."

Kostas shot to his feet. "Father, make him listen, please."

"Father agrees with me," Xander said.

"Stop!" Ari ordered. The Alpa of the Lykos pack stood up, towering over his sons. "Stop this now."

Christina couldn't stand it anymore. Her family in danger. Mama's killers on the loose. And now her brothers fighting. She stood up and without a word, ran back to the rear of the cabin and straight to her father's private quarters.

She sank down on the bed, trying desperately to hold back the tears stuck in her throat.

"Christina?"

She looked up and saw her father standing by the door. "Papa?"

Ari padded to the bed and sat down beside her. "Tell me what's wrong."

"I..." She couldn't. The tears were choking her and she couldn't breathe.

"Tell me why you ran from your mate."

"Papa..." Great sobs racked her body as the emotions broke through, like water rushing through a dam. Ari's arms wound around her and she pressed her face to his chest, her hot tears soaking his shirt. "Papa, I couldn't ... I can't. Mama ..."

Ari stroked her back with soothing motions, letting her

cry until the sobs slowed down and she could breathe again. He kissed the top of her head. "Christina, I loved your mother more than anything in the world. She was my mate and the light died in me when your mother did." He stared into her eyes, his eyes wet. "For a while, I let the darkness consume me. The need for revenge was taking over every inch of me. But it didn't. There was the small bit of light left in me. Do you know why?"

She shook her head.

"Because of you. Because of Catherine, and Cordy, and your brothers. For years, I was destroying myself with hatred and taking you all with me. It wasn't until Catherine left..." He paused and wiped the tears from his eyes. "I realized that there was still goodness, still a bit of your mother left in this world."

"Papa..." She had never resented him for what he did, for keeping them on the island like prisoners in his driving need to protect them. When Mama died, she too had been consumed with the need for revenge. When Mama married Ari, they were finally a family. She was safe and loved, and those men had taken all of that away from her.

"Do you love him?"

"I..." She swallowed. "I think so. Yes." She did. She loved Jason.

"Then tell him. Don't let the darkness consume you."

"But it's too late, Papa. He hates me. I drugged him and I planned to run away. I told him I didn't want to be with him."

"It's not too late," he said. "Not if he really is your mate."

She stood up. "We have to go back, Papa. Turn the plane around. I have to go to him."

"We can go back," he said. "But I think I have a better idea."

CHAPTER 19

JASON WASN'T sure how long he stood there, unable to move or make a sound. The coldness that had swept over him took over his body, freezing him to the spot. When he heard the door slamming behind him, he realized that she truly was gone.

Was this what it felt like to have a mate reject you? Because it fucking sucked. He whipped around, kicking the first thing he could—the couch—his foot nearly breaking it in half.

Anger seeped inside him, and his dragon roared in pain. But he couldn't explain to his inner animal why she had rejected them. She was obsessed with finding her mother's killers and he couldn't even blame her. If it had been his mother or father or any of his siblings, he'd stop at nothing to bring them justice. He realized that even with all his power and money, he couldn't offer Christina the one thing she wanted above all else – the peace that justice would bring.

Now what? He sank down on what was left of the couch. *Go home, probably.* He couldn't keep chasing after her, not when she didn't want him. It would drive him mad. But not having her was bound to also. Was this what it was going to be like the rest of his life? Feeling that empty hole in his heart and never being able to fill it?

When he finally composed himself, Jason left the safe house and made his way back to his hotel. As soon as he finished packing, he found and booked the first flight out of Heathrow, which was leaving late that evening. Good. He was glad to be getting out of this place.

―――――

The small regional plane landed on the tarmac with a bump, waking Jason up with a jolt. The captain announced their arrival in Colorado and as soon as the plane stopped at the gate, he unbuckled his seatbelt and grabbed his bag from the overhead compartment.

He hadn't brought any check-in luggage, so he went straight to Arrivals. He didn't call anyone for a ride, not really wanting to deal with having to explain what had happened. It would be just as easy take a cab or rent a car at the airport to get back to his apartment. All he wanted was to collapse into bed.

As he exited Arrivals, he searched for the taxi stand when something caught his eye.

A black truck was parked right by the door. It looked familiar. In fact, it wasn't just any truck. It was *his* truck. And, leaning on the side, arms crossed casually over her chest, was Christina.

At first he thought he was hallucinating, the lack of sleep and food playing with his head. Or maybe it was Catherine. But no. His dragon knew it, even before he did. It knew all this time.

Mine. Ours. Mate.

"Need a ride?" she asked.

"Christina?" He dropped his bag at his side and crossed the distance between them. "It's you."

"Yes. It's me. I—"

He wrapped his arms around her, feeling the softness and warmth of her body, and breathed in her sweet scent. Instinctively, his lips found their way to hers, crushing them in a sweet, slow kiss. When he finally pulled away, she looked up at him with warmth radiating in her eyes.

"I'm sorry, Jason. For what I did. For what I said. I was so consumed by my need to find Mama's killers that I didn't see what I had with you. Please forgive me."

"There's nothing to forgive. You're my mate. And I love you."

Her lips parted in surprise. "I love you too, Jason. And I want to be yours."

He brought his mouth down for another kiss. This time, an electric shock shot between them and a strange sensation seemed to spread through his body. It was calming, but at the same time exciting. Like something big was happening. Although he couldn't describe what it felt like, he knew what it was. The melding of their souls together.

"I..." She blinked.

"The mating bond," he said. "You're mine, forever."

"And *you're* mine," she said, her eyes shiny with tears.

"Let's go home," he said.

"Home to Blackstone," she finished. "But only if I get behind the wheel. I wouldn't want my driver getting us lost."

He laughed and kissed her cheek. "You can do whatever you want, just as long as you'll always be my mate."

"Forever," she answered.

CHAPTER 20

JASON DIDN'T WANT to let Christina out of his sight. They went straight back to his apartment and didn't leave for a whole twenty-four hours. He didn't want to share her either, wanting to keep her to himself, so he didn't tell anyone he'd made it home.

Even though they were mated, he knew that there were many things they had to work out. This wasn't some romantic movie where they would be living happily ever after and the screen faded to black. He would do anything in his power to make sure she was happy, but he knew it wasn't going to be easy. Christina was a complicated woman, and that was one of the things he loved about her. So, he knew they would have to talk things out.

"What are you going to do now?" he asked as they lay in bed. They were having a lazy afternoon cuddle. He enjoyed feeling her naked body against his, and running his hands over her soft skin, even if they weren't making love.

"What do you mean?" she asked in a sleepy voice.

"Well, you can't sponge off me the rest of your life—ow!"

He rubbed his head where she hit him, though she had a cute grin on her face when she did it. God, was everything about her sexy and adorable? "I mean," he said, pulling her close, his voice turning serious. "Your mom's killers. The Agency."

She frowned. "My father and brothers will find the person responsible for her death and make them pay."

"What about you? You've been wanting to do that your whole life."

"Yes," she nodded. "But I have you now. I don't want to be away from you."

"And I don't want you away from me. But I also don't want you to resent me for the rest of our lives."

"I would never resent you."

He kissed the top of her head. "I want to do whatever I can to help you. Name it, I'll do it. We'll find the people responsible for your mom's death and we'll make sure she gets justice."

"Are you proposing we go on some kind of wild revenge spree?" she asked.

He laughed. "No, we're not going to go Bonnie and Clyde on anyone. Though, you would look cute in a fedora."

"Then what do you mean? How could I possibly do my work with The Agency and be here with you? Because I told you, I choose you."

"I know," he said. "But if it had been my family and I wanted to find justice, you'd support me right?"

"Of course. I love you."

"And I love you, Christina. All I'm saying is that I don't want you to feel stuck here. When The Agency finds these fuckers and you decide you want to go get your revenge, then I want to be there too."

"To protect me?" she asked.

"Yes. Those bastards also tried to kill me and my family. I'll want to make sure they won't ever try it again."

Her expression turned clear. "I understand. We'll do it. Together."

Jason didn't realize it, but the solution to their problem came in an unlikely form the next day.

"What?" he said in an annoyed voice as he yanked his front door open. He had been in the middle of shower sex with Christina when the doorbell rang. He'd ignored it, but when the ringing became impatient, he had no choice but to answer it.

"Jason Sinclair Lennox," Riva Lennox said as she stood in front of him, hands on her hips. "Are you ever going to leave this apartment?"

"Not if I could help it," he muttered under his breath. "Hey, Mom. What's up? Oh, you brought Sybil too."

"Jason! You're naked!" Sybil shrieked and slapped her palms over her eyes.

"Yeah, people usually shower naked," he said dryly.

"My, you took your time opening the door. I'm glad you're taking your personal hygiene seriously," Riva said, her brow raised. "But we didn't even know you'd arrived back from London."

"I landed the other day. Christina picked me up," he said smugly.

"I know," Riva said with a knowing smile. "She came to Blackstone Castle a couple of hours before you did and told us everything. We gave her the keys to your truck." She clapped her hands together. "I'm glad everything worked out and you found your mate. She's a wonderful girl."

"She is," he agreed.

"Jason?" Christina asked as she peered around from behind the door. Her hair was still wet from the shower, but she was fully dressed. "Who—oh. Riva, Sybil. Nice of you to drop by."

"We were worried when we didn't hear from you," Riva said.

"Sorry, we got…distracted." She blushed. "Please, come in. And Jason, go put on some clothes."

With an unhappy grumble, Jason trudged back to his bedroom and put on a fresh pair of jeans and a T-shirt. He considered shaving, but he loved torturing Christina with his stubble by rubbing it all over her sensitive places. And he had yet to find all of them.

"Ready?" Riva asked when he came out of the bedroom.

"Ready for what?"

"We're having lunch with your parents and my father," Christina said. "Let's go."

He wasn't looking forward to meeting Ari Stavros under the circumstances, but he supposed he should make nice.

They drove back to Blackstone Castle, Jason and Christina in his truck and Riva and Sybil in his sister's car. When they got to the dining room in the east wing, Hank Lennox and Ari Stavros were deep in conversation. They broke off when the four of them walked in.

"Glad you could finally join us," Hank said, his gaze directed at his son.

"Nice to see you, too, Dad." Jason walked over to Ari. "Sir," he said formally. "It's good to meet you again."

Dark eyes looked up at him with a steely expression. "Is that all you have to say to me, after you destroyed my townhouse and put my family in danger by traipsing through London for everyone to see?"

"Papa!" Christina said, her face mortified.

"Er ... sorry?" He cleared his throat. "I mean, my apologies, sir. I'll pay for your house. But, there was something else. I wanted to ask you something."

"And what is that?"

"For your daughter's hand in marriage," he said with a gulp. Beside him, Christina let out a gasp. "I know it's old fashioned, but I wanted to get your permission to ask her."

Ari looked at Christina, his smile wistful. "You don't need it, but you shall have it." He shook his head. "I just can't believe a Blackstone dragon is taking away another one of my daughters. You don't have a third brother hiding somewhere, do you? Let me know so I can keep my Cordelia away."

"No one age-appropriate, sir," Jason quipped. Then he turned to Christina. "This was kind of spur-of-the-moment, so I don't have a ring. But I'll fly you to any store in the world and we can pick out any ring you want. So," he got down on one knee and took her hand. "Christina Stavros, you're already my dragon's mate and my soul mate. Would you do me the honor of being my wife, too?"

Christina's jaw dropped and she took a quick gasp of air before she said, "Yes. I will marry you."

Jason got to his feet and picked her up, then kissed her tenderly. She returned his kisses with an urgent fervor before pulling away.

"Congratulations!" Riva said, her eyes shiny with tears.

"Oh. My. God." Sybil said. "You're really mates!"

Hank stood up and hugged his son, and then Christina. "Welcome to the family," he said. "I'm glad my son is finally settling down."

Christina and her father also hugged warmly, the older man almost reluctant to let her go. "May your marriage be blessed with love and many children."

"Eager to be a grandfather?" Christina quipped.

"Yes." He shook his head and laughed. "A wolf with dragonling grandchildren. Who knew?"

Hank cleared his throat. "Son, I wish you'd given us some warning before you decided to be spontaneous."

"And romantic," Riva added.

"Warning? What for?" Jason asked.

"Sit down, both of you," Hank said, his voice serious. At the change in tone, the mood turned from celebratory to somber and everyone took their seats "Ari and I have been talking since they arrived here," Hank began. "He told me everything. About the SPA and what they'd uncovered."

"You did?" Christina asked. "You've never told anyone about us."

"I know," Ari said. "But times are changing. Your brother was right. We need as much help as we can get."

"And we're going to help," Hank said. "The Lennox Foundation has enough resources to bring to this fight. This isn't just about our family, but our kind."

"We must come together and form a strong alliance," Ari said. "Which is why I'm expanding The Agency to Blackstone. And I want your help, Christina."

"Me?" she asked.

"Yes, you. Who better to establish our headquarters here than you? You've worked behind the scenes and in the field."

"But it's only been a year, Papa," she said. "How could I run it all?"

"You'll have me," Jason said, looking at her warmly. "I told you, remember? We'll do it together."

"And you'll have me and your brothers for advice," Ari added.

Christina looked floored. "I … I don't know what to say."

"Will you do it?" Ari asked.

"Of course!" she said, beaming at him. "Thank you, especially for your trust in me, Papa."

"I know you can do it," Ari said. "You've always made me proud."

Christina sniffed back the tears and Jason placed a hand over hers. "You'll do great."

"All right," Riva said, wiping the tears from her eyes. "What do you guys say we get some food? I think we've had enough excitement for one day."

Christina laughed and looked at Jason warmly. He returned her smile and squeezed her hand. Deep inside him, his dragon gave a contented snort, finally at peace and whole.

EPILOGUE

"ARE YOU SURE ABOUT THAT DRESS?" Sybil asked, her nose wrinkling. "Jason's already seen you in it, albeit accidentally."

Christina laughed, thinking about that incident. "It's fine, Sybil. I can't really imagine myself in anything else." She had tried on numerous dresses at The Foxy Bridal Boutique, but her heart really was set on that particular dress.

Catherine was right. It was her dress. She was really lucky no one else had bought it since she'd tried it on. "Or maybe, it was meant to be?" Angie had said with a wink.

"I don't think Jason was looking at the dress anyway," Kate quipped. "Though he's seen a lot more since then, huh?"

"Ew, Kate!" Sybil put her hands over her ears. "I don't want to hear about my brother's sex life."

"You're such a goody-goody," Kate snorted. "How about you, Catherine? I heard the quiet ones are the wildest in the sack."

"Well…" Catherine began.

"Ugh!" Sybil groaned. "I'm starving," she proclaimed and

pointed to the cafe across the street. "Can we get a snack, please? All this shopping is making me hungry."

The four women agreed, crossed the street, and entered the cafe. It was a self-serve coffee shop, so they lined up, ordered one by one, and waited for their order at the end of the counter. Christina was the last to order, the rest of the girls having picked up their food, and was waiting for hers when she felt a tap on her shoulder.

"Yes?" She turned around. "Oh, hello..."

"Penny," the girl said. "From The Den." She fidgeted with the bottom of her shirt and looked down. "You probably don't remember me."

"I do," Christina said, recalling the events of that night. She had meant to check on the young waitress, but she just hadn't had time. "How are you, Penny?"

"I'm fine," she answered, looking up at her with wide, green eyes. "I just ... I wanted to say..." She took a deep breath. "Thank you. For the other night. If you hadn't..." Her low lip began to tremble and her face got even paler.

Christina placed a hand on Penny's shoulder. "It was nothing. No one should have to put up with that." Anger began to surge in her. The man the other night hadn't touched her, but the way Penny reacted ... she had a bad feeling this wasn't the first time.

"You were pretty bad-ass," Penny said. "The way you dealt with that guy. Are you like, a black belt in Karate or something?"

"Something like that," she replied. An idea struck her. "You know, you can learn too, if you want. To defend yourself."

"Me?" she asked. "Oh, I couldn't. I mean, I don't have the time or money to take lessons. Plus, I'm not exactly in shape like you."

"You don't need money or to be a body builder to learn," Christina said. "I'll teach you."

"What?" Her face brightened. "Really?"

Christina nodded. "You don't have to be afraid, Penny," she said, patting the other girl's arm. "And you have every right to defend yourself."

"That's ... so nice of you," she said with a slight sniffle. "I'm just ... no one's been so nice to me lately."

Christine frowned. Penny seemed like such a sweet girl. How could anyone treat her badly? "Listen, what are you doing now?"

She held up the book in her hand. "I don't have my shift until tonight, so I like to drive in early and read here."

"Come sit with us." She pointed to the table where the girls had set up.

"Oh, I couldn't..."

"You already know everyone," Christina pointed out. "I won't take no for an answer. Besides, we can set up the details of your self-defense lessons with me." She dragged Penny to the table. "You ladies remember Penny, right?" she said as she pulled out a chair.

"Of course! Penny, my girl! My bringer of tequila! I have to thank you for my wicked hangover," Kate said, raising her coffee cup.

"Oh, I'm sorry—"

"It was a joke, girl!" Kate said. "Come and take a seat."

"Thank you," Penny said as she sat down on the empty spot on the couch between Kate and Sybil. "I don't want to intrude on your girl time or anything."

"Not at all," Sybil assured her. "Besides, we could always use more girls around here."

"I just hope we won't bore you with wedding talk," Catherine said.

"Oh, I thought your wedding was a while back?" Penny asked, confused.

"It's my wedding, actually," Christina said.

"Congratulations," Penny said. "When's the big day?"

"In three weeks," she replied. She and Jason had realized that there was no need to wait, and neither wanted a big wedding like Matthew and Catherine. They were going to do a quickie ceremony at the castle with immediate family only, then have a party at the Blackstone Hotel ballroom. It would be easier to secure the ceremony and the reception that way, should the people behind the bombing try anything again. Her father and Kostas doubted there would be another attempt, but it was better to be safe than sorry.

"That's wonderful," Penny said. "I didn't realize you were planning to get engaged."

"Neither did we," Catherine said with a snort. "I can't believe Jason asked Papa for your hand in front of you."

Christina laughed. She was still getting used to the idea of being mates, but it felt right. She didn't feel any physical changes, but it was just … different. She still felt like herself, but being around Jason was just so much better. And the sex … well, that was something else.

"Me neither, but that's Jason. Besides, when you know, you know, right?"

Catherine chuckled. "Yup, and you go with it. Or you spend some time fighting it like two stubborn goats, at least until *someone* gives you the needed push to get together."

Christina shot her twin a dirty look. As soon as she and Matthew came back from their honeymoon and she told them about her and Jason, Catherine gave her a smug look. She said they knew all along and they conspired so they would get together.

"It's so romantic," Sybil declared. "I just hope my mate will turn out to be someone nice. And handsome!"

"And sexy?" Kate added.

Sybil blushed. "Well, it wouldn't hurt."

"Ah, so you do think about sex," Kate said.

"Only with my mate!" Sybil protested.

"But how about until then? Are you really saving yourself? Don't you want to have fun before you do end up shackling yourself to just one guy?" Kate asked.

"Kate..." Sybil warned, a blush spreading across her face. "It's not that I don't ... I'm not saving myself on purpose ... or anything..."

"Ugh, you are so boring. All of you are." Kate turned to Penny. "How about you, Penny? Do you have husband? A boyfriend? Or a fuck buddy?"

Penny shook her head. "Oh no. No one like that."

"Why not?" Kate asked. "Don't tell me you haven't wanted to sample what Blackstone has to offer? You know ... shifters, right?"

She gave a nervous laugh. "I haven't had the time. I just moved back to Greenville from Houston," she said, mentioning one of the towns outside Blackstone.

"How about a crush? Someone you like."

Penny's face turned as red as her hair.

"You do!" Sybil said. "Who is it?"

"It's no one. I mean, it's silly," Penny said, but the corner of her lips were curling up into a smile that reached her blue eyes.

"What? It's not silly!" Sybil said, grabbing her hand. "Who is it?"

"Is it someone from The Den?" Kate asked. "It's not my brother is it? Because I'm going to have to throw up."

"Oh no, Nate's nice to me," she said, shaking her head, her red curls bouncing around her face. "It's not him."

"Then who?" Christina asked.

"He's ... he doesn't even know I'm alive," Penny said with a wistful sigh. "I mean, I saw him and then he bumped into me, but he totally ignored me."

"How can anyone ignore those tits and that ass?" Kate said waving at Penny's generous curves.

"What is your obsession with girls' breasts?" Christina asked in an exasperated tone.

"Seriously," Kate said. "Va-va-va-voom, girl! You should be a pinup model or something."

Penny laughed. "I don't think so, I'm too shy."

"Maybe you just need a push," Kate said.

"Maybe you'll get a mate," Sybil said. "Is he a shifter?"

"I..." Penny's eyes went wide and then she went stiff as a board. She gathered her book and her purse, slinging it over her shoulder. "I ... uh, I should go. Thanks for letting me sit with you." She turned and quickly walked to the side exit.

"Penny, wait!" Christina stood up and went after her. "What's wrong?" she asked, catching up to her as she was about to exit.

"What? N-n-nothing. I'm fine. You're too kind," she said. "You shouldn't be around someone like me." She looked down and shuffled her feet.

"What do you mean like you?"

"I mean, I'm just a waitress at a bar. A nobody. You and your friends ... you're going to marry a Lennox."

"That's ridiculous," Christina said. "We don't care about stuff like that. And I mean it about the lessons, okay?"

"I ... maybe when I have time," Penny said. "I should really go. I don't want to be late for my shift."

"I'll find you at The Den," Christina said. "And you should come to our reception."

"I—"

"Hey, baby!"

She turned toward the direction of the voice. Jason. She felt warm all over, just hearing his voice and being in the same room with him. "Listen, I..." Huh. Penny was gone. *Hmmm.* There was something about the girl ... she just couldn't put her finger on it. She seemed lonely and could use a friend. Putting Penny out of her mind for now, she walked toward her mate.

"Everything okay?" Jason asked as he slipped an arm around her waist and pulled her close.

"Yeah, I'm good now that you're here," she said, turning to face him. She rested her head on his chest, enjoying his warmth. "What are you doing here?"

"Getting tuxes with Ben and Nate," he said, jerking his thumb behind him. The two guys were sitting down at the table with the rest of the girls.

"You know, if you guys told us you were planning to get married, we wouldn't have returned the tuxes. Coulda saved us some time," Nate quipped, taking a bite out of Kate's muffin.

"Hey!" Kate protested, swiping the muffin back. "Get your own, you freeloader."

"How are you, Ben?" Christina asked.

"Huh?" Ben had a puzzled look on his face and looked like he was thinking of something.

"You okay, cuz?" Jason asked.

"Yeah ... I thought there was ... I'm fine." He scratched his head. "All good."

"How'd dress shopping go?" Jason asked.

"It went fine," she said. "The dress will be ready in a week."

"Should we move up the wedding then?" Jason said with a raised brow. "You know I can't wait until you're all mine."

She laughed. "You know my family can't make it back here that fast. Cordy has her finals. Besides," she said, before pulling him down for a kiss. The touch of his lips sent a warmth throughout her body. Was this what it was like to be bonded to a mate? To feel love and contentment all the time. She sank against him and laid her head on his chest, feeling and listening to the strong beating of his heart. "I'm already all yours."

The End

Thanks for reading! Want to read some bonus and extra scenes from this book, including some sexy scenes that are too hot to publish? Sign up for my newsletter here: http://aliciamontgomeryauthor.com/mailing-list/

You'll get access to ALL the bonus materials from all my books, two FREE contemporary novels and my **FREE** novella **The Last Blackstone Dragon,** featuring the love story of Matthew's parents, Hank and Riva.

AUTHOR'S NOTES

WRITTEN ON JANUARY 23, 2018

I really can't believe that this book is done and written! For one thing, I almost thought I wasn't going to make my deadline. The holidays were awesome, but I didn't get to write as much as I wanted. But, I somehow pushed it and got it done on time. I actually discovered a cute little cafe / restaurant / bar in my hometown that stayed open until 2 a.m. and I once stayed until closing for two nights in a row, trying to finish this book.

Believe it or not, Jason and Christina's story has been knocking around my head for at least fifteen years (as was Matthew's and Catherine's). It was originally a contemporary suspense romance I had outlined, but ultimately never got around to writing. I'm so glad I'm finally able to share this story and I never thought it would end the way it did.

Up next is Ben's story. Oh Ben … what can I say about you? From the moment I started imagining what he'd be like, I was a little bit in love with him. I do love my strong, silent alpha males (and you'll see that side of him, for sure), but I can't resist those sweet and affectionate man bears. And he's the biggest one of all! I'm right in the middle of his story and I'm loving how this one's shaping up!

As usual, do drop me a line at alicia@aliciamontgomeryauthor.com if you want to tell me what you think about my story. Or, better yet, leave me a review! It helps me find out what readers like and don't like.

Until next time!

All the best,

Alicia

PREVIEW: THE BLACKSTONE BEAR

A few weeks ago...

As Penny Bennet walked into The Den, she couldn't help but feel like it was walking into an *actual* den.

Several pairs of eyes followed her as she cut across the room, tracking her like prey. It wasn't busy, but there was a group of about six men in the corner, another group of four around a small table, and two more playing billiards. All of them had stopped what they were doing to look at her. With an audible swallow, she held her head high and continued to forward.

It's not that she'd never been around shifters before. They were plenty of them back in Houston, and, having grown up just outside Blackstone, she'd known a few of them growing up in high school. But, so many of them in one small place was intimidating. The Den, and Blackstone town itself, was a well-known haunt for their kind. Bears, wolves, big cats, and (as she'd heard) a dragon or two—lots of them lived there. She couldn't help the sliver of fear slicing through her.

Stay calm, she told herself. *They're just shifters.* Like humans, except they could turn into animals with big teeth and claws. Anyway, if she wanted this job, she would have to get used to this.

Penny cleared her throat as she approached the bar. "E-excuse me?" she called the figure with his back turned to her. "I-I—" She cleared her throat louder, hoping to get rid of the phlegm that seemed to have stuck there. "I'm looking for Mr. Grimes."

The figure turned around. "Whaddaya need with me?" The man's thick white beard covered most of his face and his eyebrows were drawn together into what Penny guessed was a permanent frown. He was wearing a red flannel shirt that stretched over his wide, barrel-like chest, and suspenders tucked into black corduroy jeans. "Who are you?"

"I'm Penny," she said with a gulp. "Penny Bennet."

His eyes lit up in recognition. "Ah, Greta's girl?" The frown on his face seemed less severe now.

She nodded. "Yeah. She's my neighbor and when I mentioned that I needed a job, she said you might be looking for a waitress."

"One of my bartenders left," he said. "Got one of my wait-resses, Heather, to fill in. But, she's doing a good job so I'm giving her the position permanently." He leaned over, clasping his meaty hands together on the countertop. "You've wait-ressed before?"

"Y-yes," she said, taking a folder out of her purse. "Here's my resume—"

"A resume?" he said with a chortle, waving the folder away. "Don't need that, girl. Just tell me about you."

Light blue eyes stared back at her, and Penny had a strange feeling wash over. She suddenly understood what 'soul-piercing' meant. Was it true what people said about shifters? Could they read your mind or tell when you're telling the truth? She'd heard rumors and seen those conspiracy videos online from anti-shifter groups, but she'd always taken them with a grain of salt. Shifters never bothered her and so she never bothered with them.

"Well ... uh, I'm originally from Greenville," she began. "And then I moved to Houston to live with my grandmother when I was sixteen." Her voice shook, and she hoped he wouldn't ask why. When he didn't, she let out a small breath of relief. "I finished high school there and well, there wasn't money for college, so I started as a hostess at this local place called Rinaldi's. It wasn't a fancy place or anything, just a nice family-run restaurant. Did that for a year and then moved to waitressing and I've been doing it for four years now."

"Do you have experience working in bars?"

"Oh yeah," she said. "My second job was at a sports bar downtown."

"Houston's a big city. Why are you back here?" he asked quickly.

"Grams died last year," she stated. "And then I got a call. My daddy got sick...," she trailed off, biting her lip and hoping he wouldn't ask anymore questions.

"Well, sounds like you have solid experience," Mr. Grimes said. "But, there's one more thing I gotta ask you. Do you think you can handle the clientele around here?"

"Huh?"

"I'm not gonna mince words with ya," he said. "I keep things as orderly as I can and no one messes with me or my people. But, a lot of these guys, they work hard over at the mines, you know? They might need to blow off steam. I can't always keep an eye on you. I need someone who can hold their own, especially when my customers are idiots."

"Oh. Mr. Grimes—"

"Tim," he corrected.

"Tim," she said. "I can handle myself." She hoped he didn't notice the tremor in her voice. "I'm a very hard worker and I've been around a lot of rowdy customers. You should see what happens when the Rockets are playing," she said with a small laugh, trying to sound casual.

Tim's expression didn't change. "And the fact that my customers are shifters doesn't scare ya?"

"Of course not," she said confidently. *There were plenty of other things in the world to be scared of,* she added silently.

Tim paused and studied at her for what seemed like a full minute. "All right then. Can you start tonight?"

"Tonight?" she squeaked.

"Yeah. I got a big party, could use the help. Unless you think you can't cut it."

She was hoping she'd have a day, but beggars couldn't be choosers. With Grams gone, so was her rent-controlled apartment in the city, and she couldn't afford the new rent on her own. She had no choice but to move back to Greenville. Daddy had left the trailer to her when he died, but there were medical bills, plus gas, water, and electricity to pay and she couldn't rely on her savings forever. Some tip money would help with her dwindling funds. "Of course I can. Thank you so much, Mr.—I mean, Tim."

He nodded to another girl who was wiping down tables. "Olive'll sort you out with the uniform. Your jeans and shoes are fine, but you need the shirt." He called Olive over and told her to bring Penny to the back. "When you're done, go ask Heather to teach you the ropes while we're not too busy."

Olive let out an exasperated sigh as her face turned sour. "C'mon, new girl, let's find you a shirt." She didn't even wait for Penny to say a word and began to walk away.

Penny followed Olive to the storage room in the back. When she got there, Olive was rooting around one of the bins, then took out a dark-colored bundle.

"Sorry, we don't have shirts in your size," she said, raising a brow at Penny's bust. "This'll have to do."

"Oh...uh, thanks," she said, feeling her face go warm. Her chest had always been a problem, in more ways than one. Olive handed her the shirt, shrugged and left her alone.

Penny wasn't sure if she was meant to change in the storage room, but since the other girl didn't offer to bring her to a change room, she took off her blouse and slipped the shirt on. It was definitely snug around the chest and stretched the logo a bit, but it fit. She fluffed her red curls into place and straightened her shoulders.

This wasn't so bad, she told herself as she walked out. It was better than having to find work back in Greenville. She really didn't want to have to go back and face all the people in her hometown again. But with all those medical expenses, there was no money to take her anywhere else. She was stuck. But, she wasn't going to feel sorry for herself.

"No siree," she said under her breath. Grams would be turning over in her grave. The old woman was a tough bird and taught Penny to suck it up. Ironically, if Grams were around, she'd be the first one to tell Penny to stop thinking about her.

Tim was gone, but now there was a blonde woman wiping

down the bar top. "Hi," she said to the woman. "I'm Penny. I'm the new waitress."

"Oh, hello Penny," the bartender said with a bright smile. She wiped her hands on her jeans and offered it to her. "I'm Heather. Nice to meet ya."

She shook it. "Tim said to come talk to you when I'm done changing."

"Right," Heather said. "Well, let me show you what you need to do and introduce you to the rest of the crew."

Heather turned out to be much more personable than Tim and nicer than Olive. When she introduced her to Olive, the other woman snapped, "We've met," then walked away.

"Sorry about Olive being a bitch face," Heather said.

Penny giggled. "She's what my grams would have called a 'lemon face'." In polite company, maybe. Grams would definitely have called Olive a bitch face.

Heather laughed. "Ha! She does look like she sucked on a lemon." She sighed. "Don't worry, she'll get over it."

"Over what?"

"Well…" Heather lowered her voice. "If you ask me, she's pretty disappointed that one of the former employees here, Catherine, snagged a Lennox."

"A what?"

"A Lennox. Particularly, Matthew Lennox."

"Who's that?" Penny asked.

"Oh, you're not from Blackstone, are you?"

She shook her head.

"Well, let me give you the short version. The Lennoxes are a family of dragons who founded Blackstone. They own the blackstone mines and they're richer than sin," Heather said. "And Matthew's like, the head honcho of Lennox Corporation. Anyway, he met Catherine, who used to be the bartender here, and fell head over heels for her. It's a very long story but," she nodded to the banner above the bar which read 'Congratulations Matthew and Catherine', "tonight's their engagement party. And bitch face just can't accept that Matthew chose Catherine, especially after she's been shaking her perky little titties at him since she started here."

Penny chuckled. "Oh my. I guess I'd be bitchy-faced too if that happened to me." Though she didn't mean it, it seemed like the right thing to say.

Heather looked down at her chest. "I don't know, I think if any man saw those first..."

Penny went red.

"Don't worry, I'll order a larger size for you. Now, let me show you how to get the tab out..."

Heather was a patient teacher and Penny was grateful for the help. It wasn't anything she hadn't done before, but the system was slightly different from the sports bar back in Houston. But she knew the only way to learn was to do it, so she plunged in head first, immediately taking her first order as soon as Heather went back to slinging drinks.

After a few hours, The Den was starting to get crowded. It was a Saturday night after all. And really, it wasn't that much different from any bar anywhere else. If anything, Penny actually felt safer here, especially with Tim keeping a watchful eye over everything. Sure, a lot of the men's gazes would linger a little too long on her chest or she could feel them staring at her ass while she walked away or a couple would call her "sweetie" or "honey", but no one tried anything inappropriate. And shifters were damned good tippers. She was already skipping happily, thinking of how much she'd be taking home tonight.

As Penny was heading back to the bar to grab another

round of drinks, a cheer erupted behind her, along with the sounds of poppers and confetti guns.

"Happy couple's here," Heather said pointing to the door.

As she glanced back, she saw a man and woman surrounded by well-wishers. "Oh my." They were a beautiful couple—he was tall, dark-haired and handsome, while the woman was willowy, slim and gorgeous. They were like the prom king and queen striding in to greet their subjects. No wonder poor Olive was so sour.

"Need help with those?" Heather asked, looking at the full tray.

"I'm fine," she said, a bit embarrassed at being caught staring. "I'll be right back."

Penny lifted the tray and walked over to the table, dispensing the drinks easily. One of the tables stopped her, and she took their orders. As she walked away, something very solid bumped into her.

As she began to fall back, she braced herself, ready for her butt to hit the floor. However, a pair of hands grabbed her arms, stopping her from tumbling over. *Oh my ...* Something, no *someone*, smelled so *good*. The cologne was heady and male and fresh. As she looked up, she saw a handsome face covered with a thick beard looking ahead past the crowd of people behind her. Or rather, over her head, as the man was gigantic, especially compared to her petite frame. A small sound escaped her as she felt her feet lift off the ground. The man had picked her up and placed her aside, then went on his merry way.

"Eeep!" She covered her mouth as soon as the squeak came out. She stared after the man, watching his large back retreating from her. A shiver ran through her, thinking of his warm, calloused palms on her bare arms. *What happened?*

She watched him join a table—not just any table, but *the* table—the one where the newly engaged couple was holding court with their friends and family. *Of course.* The man who bumped into her was hunky and gorgeous and he was one of them, the elite of Blackstone. *He didn't even look at me.* Why would he? She was just a waitress after all.

Shaking off imaginary dust from her jeans, she walked back to bar. "Two rum and cokes and a whiskey," she said to Heather.

"You okay?" the other woman asked with a frown. "You're redder than a firetruck."

Penny touched her cheek, which was indeed warm. "I'm fine." She glanced over at the table again and she saw the man laughing with his friends. It made him seem even more handsome, the way he seemed so relax and genuine.

"Oh, Ben's here," Heather said, following her gaze. "I didn't see him come in."

"Do you know him?"

"Well, not personally, but sure, everyone knows him. He's head of the mining operations and related to the Lennoxes. Cousins or something."

"Right." So, handsome, popular *and* rich. Of course he wouldn't notice someone like her. Girls were probably throwing themselves at him. Why would he notice someone like her?

Penny shook her head. No use thinking about that. "You got those drinks for me?"

"Coming right up."

Available now on Amazon!

Made in the USA
Las Vegas, NV
27 November 2023

81685491R00121